KOA'S LITTLE GIRL

PEPPER NORTH

Copyright © 2025 by Stormy Night Publications and Pepper North

All rights reserved. No part of this book may be reproduced or transmitted in any form or by any means, electronic or mechanical, including photocopying, recording, or by any information storage and retrieval system, without permission in writing from the publisher.

Published by Stormy Night Publications and Design, LLC.
www.StormyNightPublications.com

North, Pepper
Koa's Little Girl

Cover Design by AllyCat's Creations

This book is intended for *adults only*. Spanking and other sexual activities represented in this book are fantasies only, intended for adults.

CHAPTER 1

"Look, military hotshot, based on the height of those flames, I could charge you with arson. I don't know if you're dimwitted or totally incompetent, but you risked your home and the homes of the other hard-working people in the area," the fire captain told him with anger radiating from her gaze.

Koa backtracked immediately, dropping his charming smile that usually smoothed over any disagreement with the opposite sex. She was not receptive to flirting at all. He switched to all business trying to dig himself out of the hole he found himself almost buried in. "Yes, ma'am. You are absolutely correct. I should have never started my teammate's grill without him being here to clue me in about its operation. Thank you for coming to assist."

"Assist? You mean put out the roof-high fire flare," she corrected him, visibly bristling more at his use of that word.

Koa had regretted his wording immediately when he saw her react to it. He backtracked again. "You are totally correct. Our fire extinguishers did not faze the flames. Your firefighters saved the day."

"You bet your ass they did. Don't let it happen again or I will cite you."

. . .

Replaying the previous evening's conversation with the fire captain on an endless loop had interrupted his sleep last night. By the morning, he'd already decided he needed to mend fences, or at least, apologize one more time. Not only did Koa know she was right, he needed to see her to double-check his reaction. He'd picked up something special about that woman.

Throwing on fatigues and a T-shirt for that day's training, he headed to the fire station. He left his car in the parking lot and headed across the asphalt driveway. With luck, she would still be on duty. As he approached, a couple of guys paused from their chore of sweeping out the bay.

"Can we help you, sir?" one called.

"I'm looking for Giana Mancini. Is she working today?" Koa asked, glancing around.

"She's here. Who are you?" the other said suspiciously.

Instantly, Koa knew they were interested in the stunning captain. "Would you tell her that the wingman last night wishes to see her?"

"Wingman? She's not going to understand that," the man said, glaring at Koa.

Something in his tone that made Koa take a hard look at him instead of a fleeting glance. Physically fit, of course, the blond firefighter's expression was anything but welcoming to a visitor. The glare he leveled at Koa felt personal.

"Wait! Are you the guy who started a ten-foot-high flame in a gas grill last night?" the dark-haired one asked, drawing Koa's attention away from the first man. This guy's demeanor was completely different as he grinned and shook his head in disbelief.

"Yeah. My teammate's grill. I should have waited for him to get home," Koa admitted. The team had ribbed him all day about the wing fiasco. While it had been good-natured teasing, he was starting to bristle when they brought it up now.

"You think?" a woman's voice mocked him from behind.

Koa turned to meet beautiful brown eyes. "Definitely. I'd hoped to talk to you. Can I steal a bit of your time?" When she hesitated and glanced at the men working in the outside bay, he suggested, "Let's stand under that big oak tree on the edge of the drive."

"Why?"

"I thought we got off to a rough start," Koa said, walking forward. When she crossed her arms over her chest, he immediately halted, not wishing to push past her comfort zone. *Damn! She's even prettier without the heavy protective gear.* He swallowed hard in reaction as something inside him clicked into place. Koa hadn't imagined his attraction to her last night.

To his surprise, she nodded and walked past him to the spot he'd indicated. When they reached the shade, she turned to face him with a hard stare. "What do you want?"

"To apologize. I'm sorry for losing control of the fire. That could have had a bad ending."

She stared at him as if assessing his honesty for several seconds before answering, "Mistakes happen. That's what we're here for."

"I'm Koa," he introduced himself, holding out his hand.

"I'm not interested," Giana answered bluntly. She didn't extend her hand. She glanced past Koa to the line of male firefighters who stood watching their exchange.

When Koa followed the line of her view, he noted their expressions ranged from casual interest to anger. *That blond guy has judged me as competition.* Koa was okay with that. He was here for a reason.

When he turned to Giana once again, her expression had hardened further to pure granite. It didn't take a genius to figure out what was happening here. She had very consciously separated business from pleasure. Some guys had accepted that. One had not.

"This doesn't seem like a good place to talk. Where do you usually hang out when you're not at the station?" Koa asked.

"Look. I accept your apology, Conan," she told him. "Just don't create any more charcoal wings."

"Koa."

"What?" she asked, her eyebrows drawing together in confusion. Was he making it up, or did her eyes reveal that her bumble was deliberate?

"My name is Koa."

"Right. Koa. We've got a lot to do around the firehouse. If you'll excuse me."

"Where's the best coffee in town?" he asked on impulse.

"Krieger's on Main," she answered automatically.

"Thank you, Giana." Koa nodded. "Tell me, who's the tall blond guy on the end?"

"Why?" she asked, her eyes narrowing at him.

"I always listen to my intuition," he answered honestly. Something about that guy set off warning signals in his brain. A shadow passed over Giana's face, and he suspected she had the same sense about him.

"Tom, stop standing around and hand me the wrench, please," a voice requested from the open bay.

Koa turned to see a firefighter back at work, fixing a panel on an ambulance. The glowering blond reached into a toolbox and handed the tool over before returning to scrutinizing Koa and Giana.

"Tom. Watch out for him, Giana." Koa didn't wait for her to answer, but returned to his truck, shouting, "Be safe," to the firemen still working outside. *Nothing to see here. Simply a grateful citizen.*

The last thing he wanted to do was to cause his little girl trouble at the station. He already suspected that her rise to captain had been hard-fought. Shocked, Koa repeated that phrase to himself. *His little girl.* His brain didn't have any doubt that she was his or, despite all her bravado, that she was a Little. Koa didn't have a clue how he knew. He just did.

Grinning, he started his truck and drove out of the fire station's parking lot. He'd have some work to do, but he'd never run from a challenge. Stubborn, his mother had called him. Koa preferred to call himself determined. That trait, whatever it was, had helped him achieve a position on the Special Forces team.

The image of his unit ribbing him over the wing fiasco last night made his lips twitch upward again. They'd saved his life a half a dozen times already. As the communications soldier on the team, he was a huge target for any opposing force. Take him out, and the entire team was isolated.

Koa knew each man on the team would risk his life to save his—not because of the radio he carried. He'd give his for them as readily as well. They survived together, or didn't.

Pulling into the base, Koa drove to the training building Jerico had arranged as their equipment space. After Jerico had been chosen by the last team leader, Koa had slowly accepted his authority. The newest member of the team had shown his dedication, skills, and intelligence repeatedly. The way Jerico had zeroed in on Aspen and saved her from being terrorized by her brute of a neighbor had shown Koa Jerico's true character.

As he parked, Koa caught sight of his team gathered outside with packs on their backs. *Damn.* Caden had a tough day planned for them. He slid out of his truck and jogged forward.

"Good timing," Caden called and slung Koa's pack toward

him. As soon as Koa caught it, Caden ordered, "Go grab your practice firearm."

Without a second's pause, Caden said, "Hank, you take lead."

Instantly, the quietest member of the team ran for the tree line. Koa swore and shrugged into his pack, racing inside to unlock the training locker and retrieve the weapon he used in training. The team had disappeared from view when he returned.

Speeding in the direction he'd seen them last, Koa sprinted to catch up with the others. A snapping twig helped him get oriented. When Koa reached the group, he automatically fell into step and shot a thankful look at Max. The big man nodded, confirming what Koa had guessed. He'd deliberately broken the debris to signal Koa.

The team ran in perfect harmony, their breaths slow and controlled. Each stride of their protective combat boots landed quietly in the dirt. They trained to achieve the ultimate athletic performance—one that would help ensure their survival in the worst conditions.

After five miles, Caden sped up to take the lead, relieving their sniper from setting the pace. Caden immediately flashed a hand signal that every member of the team followed. Within a couple of seconds, they'd faded into deeper foliage. Like usual, Caden directed them with gestures, and the team divided into two. Koa stuck with Jerico. Max, the team's bomb expert, joined them.

Operating blind since he'd missed the team meeting, and they were under orders for silence, Koa could only guess that Max had a pivotal part in today's exercise. The radio pack sent an unmistakable thump against his spine, silently alerting him. Without hesitating, Koa stopped in his tracks and signaled the target location to Max. Caden had obviously activated target locations in the radar of his communication pack.

They moved through the woods noiselessly, stopping only when Koa located a new spot. As always, he studied Max's skilled hands setting up the detonation charges. The large man's dexterity impressed him. Koa would move from being the communications guy to another skilled position on the team as he gained experience. Rarely did a team need two bomb experts, but someone to help in a pinch was always a bonus.

The sound of gunfire echoed under the canopy of the trees. Birds flew in a flurry of sound and color. A specific firing pattern identified the attackers. The other half of Koa's team pushed the enemy back toward the charges. They needed to finish their job quickly.

To Koa's surprise, in the next location, Max thrust a supply of materials toward him and pointed to a large pile of rocks to their right. Koa didn't hesitate. Following the steps he'd memorized watching training videos and seeing Max in action, Koa quickly set up a powerful explosion. When Max's mass approached, Koa slid out of the way. Max altered Koa's setup slightly and gave him a thumbs-up.

The trio moved out of the blast zone and waited, ready to surprise anyone who survived the explosions. The first flares went up, representing the first bombs igniting. Koa spotted a bunny running from his right. At his signal, the trio moved away, finding a better location. They didn't question his input.

Being trusted felt good.

A small group burst into their recently vacated area. Koa didn't have time to celebrate for heeding his intuition earlier. From their new sheltered location, Max, Jerico, and Koa eliminated them as Max triggered the last charges, sending up flares. That took out the last surviving attackers.

When the other team leader conceded their defeat, Koa's team reunited without celebration. They weren't arrogant or gloating. This training mission would hopefully prepare them to survive a real-life skirmish. The team would celebrate that win. Koa watched Caden and Jerico walk forward to meet with the other troop's leadership.

"Any injuries?" Zale asked the team. When he had everyone's assurances they were fine, Zale moved forward to help the other troop's medic.

With fake charges and rubber bullets, the damage was minimal. The morale of the larger group that hadn't succeeded in its mission took the biggest hit. Koa spotted a familiar face: a soldier he'd met in training who hadn't landed a Special Ops position yet. He walked forward to greet him.

"You all dogged us," Mark said, pulling Koa into a one-armed bro hug.

"That move to the side was smart. You almost got us there," Koa shared.

"But not quite. Had I moved my section earlier, I would have had you," Mark said.

"Maybe," Koa hedged. The possibility he wouldn't have noticed earlier existed—barely. "A bunny gave you away."

"Fuck! Of course it did," Mark laughed. Natives could always throw a monkey wrench into a great plan.

After debriefing the conflict thoroughly with the other troops, Caden called the team back together. "Let's get out of here. Koa earned a beer on me tonight. But we've got miles to go yet."

By the time they returned to base, everyone dripped with sweat. Koa shrugged off his pack and collapsed to the grass with the others. When they'd all drained the last of their water, Caden targeted Koa with an assessing look.

"What delayed you this morning?"

"I made a stop at the firehouse to apologize," Koa said, striving for a casual tone.

"To apologize?" Max focused on that bit of information. "To whom?"

"My bet's on the fire captain," Jerico said.

"She was not into you at all," Zale chimed in. "So, how did it go?"

"I apologized and hightailed it here to go hang out in the woods with you losers," Koa answered, ribbing his team.

"But we weren't losers," Max said. "Good work on the explosives. Yours would have worked as you shaped it. Mine was just better."

"Thanks. I'm trying to figure out whose job I'm coming after. I'd try for Jerico's, but he's in too many meetings," Koa said.

"Speaking of… I have to shower and change before I go do battle over our budget. Maybe I need to learn to 'shape' explosives." Jerico always kept his tone light, but the others on the team recognized how hard he worked to get the leadership to spring for what they needed.

"Here. I hid a candy bar in my pack for secret energy," Koa said, pulling out a Snickers.

"Keep it. I need to watch my girlish figure," Jerico said with a laugh. "I don't want Aspen to start counting my gut rolls instead of my abs." He eyed Koa's flat stomach as if he noticed a few extra pounds.

"Get out of here with your buff body. I could beat you at sit-ups any day," Koa challenged.

"Thanks, guys. I was just thinking about how we should train tomorrow. Old-fashioned calisthenics it is," Caden announced.

Groans filled the air. It was one thing to run an obstacle course or take part in a staged encounter like today. But a day filled with endless exercise in the gym was a killer. Especially if it was a competition among their team. None of them would ever give up.

"There's a sadistic streak in you, isn't there, Caden?" Max asked.

"It's taken you this long to figure me out?" Caden joked.

Koa rolled his eyes and peeled back the wrapper of his treat. He was usually very exacting with nutrition, but sometimes everyone needed pure, empty calories. "Anyone up for a night out?"

"Not me. I promised to make cheesy spaghetti for one little girl tonight," Jerico said with a smile.

"I'm out, too. Pippa's classroom is having a singalong with their parents this afternoon. I promised to go watch," Zale explained. His little girl worked at the on-base daycare. "Pray for everyone that they don't ask me to carry a melody."

"No one is ready for that," Hank said with a shake of his head. "I'm working on my place. Anyone who's free can come help pull up carpet."

"Count me in. I don't have a life," Max answered.

"I'll help," Koa volunteered. "I'll even stop and pick up some coffee for everyone."

"You don't even drink coffee," Zale pointed out.

"So?" Koa answered. "I may have to take up the habit."

CHAPTER 2

*W*hoever invented an Americano with two shots of espresso should be a millionaire. Giana yawned behind a polite hand and tried to keep her toe from tapping impatiently as she waited. She had ordered after the flashy young woman ahead of her had finished batting her eyelashes at the barista. Giana thrust a hand through her work-rumpled hairdo and remembered dressing up to be seen and admired. She was not attracting the same level of attention as the blonde dazzler. *Priorities definitely change with time and responsibilities.*

Customers packed the coffee shop in the early evening. She loved this place for the great coffee and the range of customers. Everyone from elderly couples to teenagers already addicted to caffeine filled the shop. Giana had found a spot close enough to hear the barista yell names, but far enough away to avoid the crush of people hoping their order would be crafted next.

"Order for Lookaloo!" the barista called.

No one moved.

"Lookaloo?"

When no one stepped forward to take the cup, she tried, "Three pumpkin spice latte frappes?"

A muscular man stepped into her line of sight and claimed the milkshake-like concoctions in a cardboard carrier. He didn't fit the image she had of the average pumpkin spice frappe drinker. Giana controlled her expression with effort as she laughed inside. And his name? Lookaloo? Poor guy. Thank goodness he didn't work at the fire station.

Crap! Giana glanced down immediately as the buff man turned to face her. She recognized the man who'd come to see her this morning.

"Hey, fancy meeting you here," Koa said, stopping in front of her.

That was all she could take. Her mouth quivered with merriment. "Lookaloo?"

"Yeah, it took me a minute to figure out they'd butchered my name. It's actually Lokela. It's Hawaiian."

"Do you drink a lot of pumpkin spice?"

"Are you the coffee police?" Koa lifted the cup to his mouth and stopped, realizing he needed a straw.

That was the final blow. Her control totally evaporated. Giana shielded her mouth with one hand as she giggled. She tried never to laugh around anyone other than family. Her amusement sounded like a delighted seven-year-old. It hadn't changed since then. His answering smile told her he'd noticed.

Giana spoke quickly to distract him. "I thought you Special Forces guys treated your bodies like a temple?"

"Noticed my physique, did you?" Koa teased.

Immediately back on the defensive, Giana pushed back her shoulders to stand at her full 5′5″ height. She'd grown up with five brothers. Giana had learned to go toe to toe with any of them. She never backed down from a fight.

"Hey, I'm sorry. I thought we were joking with each other. You're right. I do watch my diet carefully," Koa assured her.

She eyed him, trying to figure the soldier out. Something was different about him. "I bet. Nutrition is important."

"Giana? An Americano with double espresso?" the barista called.

Koa looked at her as he absorbed her order. Less sugar than his, but an insane amount of caffeine.

She held up a hand and shook her head. "I know—the proverbial pot calling the kettle black, right? A coffee shop is a nonjudgmental zone. Excuse me. I'll go grab that."

Giana weaved her way through the gathered customers and claimed her drink. Tightening her resolve, she headed for the door. *Time to leave.*

As she opened the door, she spotted him waiting for her outside. Koa had anticipated her actions once again. First her coffee run and now her escape. "I'm not interested, okay?" she told him bluntly.

"Gotcha. I wanted to thank you for the coffee shop recommendation. It's hard to find good…" His voice died away as he waved a hand over the drinks he'd ordered.

"Pumpkin spice latte frappes?" she suggested.

"Exactly. I don't suppose you know a good hairstylist?" he asked, rubbing his hand over his military-short stubble.

She rolled her eyes at him, charmed by his quick wit and willingness to make fun of himself. Giana lifted her hand and said a quick, "Bye!" before heading to her truck. Time to go home.

"See you later, Flame."

She kept herself from turning back to glance at him. Why did that sound like he'd given her a nickname? And why did she get the impression Koa wasn't fooled by the polished persona she showed the world?

Giana studiously didn't look back at him as she left the

parking lot. Something about Koa Lokela that captured her attention. Whatever it was, she'd avoid it like wildfire.

Pulling into her apartment complex, she navigated to her assigned parking spot. *Oh, great.* Her next-door neighbor's boyfriend already occupied it. Giana crossed her fingers, hoping they'd choose to go to his house. The paper-thin walls didn't block their vigorous activities.

Just what she needed after her regular twenty-four-hour shift—Veronica's headboard banging into the wall that separated them. Giana didn't need to be reminded of how long it had been since she'd had a guest with benefits. She'd decided at the beginning of her career not to date a firefighter. Complications and jealousy could run rampant inside the building.

Giana preferred the men to view her as the captain rather than a potential girlfriend. It had taken months to convince everyone that she wasn't interested—even in them. After Koa's visit, she'd had to fend off three requests for dates.

Koa. What was it about the Special Forces soldier?

This close to base, she was used to military guys. They were always in incredible shape. Koa seemed even more... He'd focused only on her. The flashy blonde teenager in abbreviated shredded shorts and a halter top hadn't caught his eye at all, despite the virtual drool on the floor from the other men in the coffee shop.

Those dark brown eyes seemed to see past all the barriers she'd created to guard her inner self. The dark shadow of his whiskers after a long day made her imagine what the handsome man would look like with a full beard. The scruff was attractive. After not shaving for a week, he would be a walking billboard for a testosterone overload.

A honk behind her made Giana realize she was idling in the middle of the parking lot. With an 'I'm sorry' wave, she pulled into a guest parking spot and turned off her engine.

The horn blared a second time with indignation, and the inconvenienced driver didn't move. Rolling her eyes, Giana stepped out of her car.

"You need to learn how to drive!" the jerk behind the wheel of a blue sedan yelled as he glared daggers at her.

"Sorry, sir. A long day at work. My apologies for holding you up," Giana said and headed for her apartment building.

"We all have long days at work, bitch."

Giana kept walking and took a sip of her coffee to stop herself from popping off with an equally rude response. She refused to allow the man to rile her. Waving her key fob at the security door, she walked into her building and pushed the door closed behind her. She'd be careful going in and out for the next few days. That hothead would soon shift his anger to someone else.

Taking a second to claim her mail from the entryway, Giana couldn't wait to get in the shower and unwind a bit before going to bed. She'd become a firefighter to help others, but some days her job was a bit too people-y.

Once in her apartment, she locked the door and deadbolt. She dropped off the rest of her drink at her favorite spot on the sofa before heading for the shower. For many, drinking caffeine before bed would make them toss and turn for hours. Giana lived on the delicious brew at all hours. She'd learned to sleep when she could because the next emergency could sound at any time.

After letting the water pelt down on her tired muscles, Giana pulled on her favorite nightshirt and stepped into her bunny slippers. She padded out to the living room and pulled the vertical blinds across the sliding glass doors on the balcony. The room darkened immediately, and she asked her virtual personal assistant to turn on the light.

With a sigh of relief, Giana crawled onto her modular sectional sofa. She loved this U-shaped monstrosity with ottomans cuddled up to it. It was the closest thing to having a crib that looked normal to anyone who visited. She carefully picked up Jellybean from the nest the stuffie had napped in while Giana was at work and settled on the pile of pillows. Jellybean was a new acquisition, but she loved her lots.

"Hi, Jelly! I missed you. Did anything exciting happen here?" Giana asked the sweet creature.

She listened carefully to Jelly's answer and nodded. "The office sent out a notice last week that they were going to come in to check the air filters. The maintenance guy didn't scare you, did he? Yeah, he's nice. I like him too. Want to watch a movie?"

After listening to the stuffie's answer, she cheered, "Perfect! That's a brilliant choice."

Giana squirmed on the couch to reach the remote and started the movie she'd seen a million times before. Singing along with the dancing animals, she and Jelly enjoyed it for the million and first time. When the credits ended, she was too lazy to move. After turning everything off, she grabbed a throw from the back of the couch and crashed into sleep.

* * *

"Please. Please, Daddy," Giana begged.

Jolted out of an erotic dream by the sound of her own voice, Giana stilled and blinked into the darkness. She ached with desire. *Damn him.* Koa's face lingered in her mind. *He's not a daddy.*

Or is he? Her imagination battled with her skeptical nature. She'd searched for a daddy for so long and not found one. Why was this guy sticking in her brain?

She untangled herself from the soft material trapped around her legs. Her fingertips brushed over her mound, leaving an electric zing that lingered from the soft touch.

Giana spread her legs as she pulled up her nightshirt. She traced the cleft of her pussy, finding herself slick.

An image of Koa popped into her mind as she stroked herself more intimately. His powerful form inspired her fantasies. What would he look like naked?

Her imagination's Koa yanked his fitted T-shirt over his head and drew his fingers down his chiseled torso. When he popped open the top button of his fatigues, Giana glided her fingers through her wetness to trace her opening. She shivered as her body responded eagerly.

Picturing him in her mind, she watched him slowly finish releasing his pants, revealing his thick cock. Giana slid two fingers into her drenched pussy as she dreamed of how his shaft would stretch her. A soft moan fell from her lips as she flicked her thumb over her clit. She wouldn't last long. Just talking to him briefly had put her on edge.

In her vivid fantasy, Koa crawled on his hands and knees toward her and stopped to wrap his fingers around himself. "Let's have a contest, little girl. Who can hold out the longest? The person who comes first gets her bottom spanked," he explained the rules as he jerked his hand down his cock.

That threat was all it took to push her over the edge. Giana cried out as she exploded with pleasure and shook. She lightened her touch and then pulled her hands away when even that was too much. Koa faded from her mind, and she blinked into the empty room. Her stuffed bunny stared back at her with knowing plastic eyes.

"He's a daddy, Jelly. I know he has to be. Can you help me be brave enough to take a risk?"

Did Jelly just wink at her? Giana grabbed her new best friend and hugged her close. With her stuffies in her corner, Giana might be able to try.

CHAPTER 3

The next day in the middle of a set of three hundred sit-ups, Jerico's phone went off. They all froze at the sound of the tone Jerico had programmed in to notify him that there was a message from the base. Only Jerico and Caden carried phones during training for emergencies. Everyone else stored theirs in their lockers.

"Jerico, get that. Everyone else, keep going unless you want to do another set," Caden ordered.

Jerico rolled away from the ground and rose to walk a few feet away. He answered the phone as everyone strained to finish the exercise and eavesdrop at the same time. "Koa? Yes, he's here training. Okay. I'll tell him."

Without saying anything else, Jerico rejoined the group and upped his pace to make up for the thirty seconds he'd missed. Koa waited for him to explain why his name had come up. Jerico said nothing, but continued to do his workout.

"Two minutes to rest and then plank," Caden announced.

"Jerico, what's up?" Koa asked.

"Oh, there's a letter from a sexy woman at the front gates for you," Jerico answered.

Koa stared at him in disbelief as the other men hooted, applauded, or both. "What?"

"A beautiful brunette just drove up and left an envelope for you at the front guard shack. She didn't have clearance or an appointment, so they couldn't let her in," Jerico reported. "They notified me you can pick it up whenever convenient."

"Giana. It has to be her," Koa guessed. He whirled to look at Caden, hoping to get permission to go.

"No way, Koa. You'll be mush for the rest of the day. They'll hold on to it for you. You can pick it up at lunch," Caden told him.

"You're kidding, right?" Koa stared at the older man in disbelief.

"I am. Come on. I think we'll hold off on that plank challenge until we have a sprint for the guard shack. What do you say? The first soldier there gets to read Koa's letter aloud?" Caden suggested.

Koa sprinted out the door before the team chief finished. The others were on his heels as they pelted down the hallway and out the front door. Jabbing Hank in the side with his elbow as the sniper tried to pass him, Koa took advantage of Hank's stumble to the side to stay in the lead. There was no way anyone would get to read that letter before him.

The guards stood outside the shack watching them come. Koa didn't care that he'd become the day's entertainment. He wanted that letter now. *Please let it be her.* He hadn't been able to get her out of his mind.

"Hey, Koa. I guess you got the message," the guard said with a smile as he handed over a long white envelope.

"Thanks," Koa said, holding it away from his sweating body.

He turned to walk back to his team, who waited a few feet

away. They all smiled broadly at him. Koa realized they hadn't truly attempted to win. They'd just made him work for it.

"Going to read it?" Zale asked.

"Later," Koa told him. He wanted to have privacy to process whatever Giana written. *Please don't let her tell me to fuck off.*

"Alright! If you all are finished slacking off, let's head for that field," Caden directed and took off running. "We can hold that plank in the fresh air. You guys are getting too fragrant for the gym."

Koa scooped up a clean-looking stone from the ground. He'd need something to work as a paperweight while they trained. Soon, he balanced on his forearms as he stared down at the white envelope. His mind whirled so much with the possibilities, Koa won the competition without realizing it. He dropped to the grass when he noticed everyone had collapsed.

Thanks, little girl. She was already bringing him good luck.

* * *

BY THE END of the day, the crisp envelope was battered and bruised. Koa had carried it with him throughout their activities today. It looked as worn as his team.

"Dismissed," Caden announced.

Koa didn't hesitate. He grabbed the envelope and pelted toward his locker to get his keys and phone. Raising a hand to acknowledge the calls from the team wishing him good luck, Koa concentrated on reaching his truck to open the letter in private.

There, he unsealed the envelope carefully and pulled out a single sheet of white paper.

Are you a daddy?
  G

He reread the question three times, trying to convince himself it was real. When he trusted what he saw, Koa checked the time and drove toward the coffee shop. Racing to the firehouse would cause her problems. He could only hope that she would be brave enough to meet him.

When Koa turned into the parking lot, he spotted her in the window. When their eyes met through the glass, Koa's heart thumped hard in his chest. He parked and hurried to the door. He walked straight to Giana.

Pulling a chair as close as possible, he sat down and wrapped his hand around hers, which twisted on the tabletop. "Yes."

"Really? I'd started to think they didn't exist."

"I wondered if I'd ever find you. I should have sacrificed wings to the barbecue gods a long time ago," Koa said, trying to break the tension he could see stiffening her body.

"That was dangerous," she warned, regaining a bit of her fire.

"How long have you been here?" he asked.

"I figured you'd get my note on your way out. I didn't cause you any trouble, did I?" Giana asked.

"You did not. And even if you did, I couldn't care less. Thank you for being so brave. I didn't know whether you felt it too. I'd already decided to ask you this afternoon if you were here."

When she leaned slightly toward him, Koa couldn't stop himself. He slid his fingers into her thick, soft tresses and drew her forward. He kissed her lightly, nibbling at her lips until she pressed her mouth against his fully. Fighting his flaring desire, Koa ended the kiss.

The look in her eyes tested his resolve. He loved the soft glow of her happiness. "We have a lot to discuss, little girl," he told her quietly. "Can we go somewhere more private? Perhaps my house? I promise you are perfectly safe with me."

She hesitated for a second and then nodded. "Are you okay with me sending your name and address to a friend?"

Koa reached for his wallet in his back pocket and pulled out his driver's license and his military ID. After placing them on the table in front of her, he said, "Take a picture of these and send it to her. That address is correct."

She smiled and quickly followed his directions. "Can I have your number? It would be easier to contact you directly."

"Of course." Koa recited the number and had her call him to double check she had it correct. He quickly saved her number as well.

"Ugh," another customer said and moved to a table farther away with her nose in the air.

Giana's lips twitched with amusement as she tried not to laugh.

Koa leaned slightly away from the beautiful woman next to him. "I probably smell like I've done a million jumping jacks," he said as he quickly replaced his identification.

"Add a few thousand burpees," she suggested with a smirk.

He had to laugh. Her training as a firefighter was intense as well. Giana would be used to being with a group of smelly athletes. That didn't excuse his odor. "Sorry. I didn't stop to take a shower. I wanted to come find you."

"I'm glad you did. Let's go before they kick us out for spoiling the caffeine brew scent in here," Giana suggested.

Koa stood and waited for Giana to join him. Needing to touch her, he placed his hand lightly on her lower back and guided her out of the coffee shop. "I'm in that black truck," he said, pointing to his vehicle. It was wonky in the parking lot, revealing his need to get to her quickly.

"I'm over there, in *that* black truck," she told him with a laugh.

Koa shook his head in disbelief. His Little was so right for him. He couldn't wait to learn everything about her. To his delight, she stepped close and lifted her chin to ask for a kiss. Koa wrapped his hands around her waist and fought his desire to pull her tight against his post-training sweatiness as he kissed her. Her flavor and eagerness thrilled him.

Don't go too fast, he reminded himself. Her small sounds of enjoyment spoke directly to his cock. Damn, he wanted this woman badly.

He stepped back and met her gaze. "Come home with me, Giana. I need to learn everything about you."

"I'm right behind you," she promised.

CHAPTER 4

*G*iana parked her truck next to him. It was fun to see how their vehicles seemed to signal that they had a lot in common. As she slid out of her truck and landed with a gentle bump, Giana regretted the two coffees she'd consumed while waiting for him. She hadn't wanted to leave the table by the window in case he arrived.

"Now I'm hoping I didn't leave a mess inside," Koa said with a smile as he escorted her up to the door.

She loved the warmth of his hand on her back. Koa automatically took care of her. As far as she could tell, it wasn't an act. Giana definitely wasn't used to a man behaving like that.

"I promise not to judge," she assured him as he opened the door.

Good heavens! Koa's house was immaculate and sparse. Everything was in its place, and no dust would dare to land on the furniture in fear of instant annihilation. "I think you're safe. And I know you're never coming to my house if you think this is messy."

"Military training," he explained. "Plus the fact I don't spend much time here."

"Oh, are you a bar fly?"

"I do like music and dancing. But I spend a lot of time with my team."

"You Special Forces guys seem to hang around each other," Giana observed.

"We do. This is my first team so I can't comment on how close other groups are, but when your life depends on those other guys, you bond."

"I bet. Go get cleaned up. I'll be fine here," Giana urged as she took a seat on the couch.

"Please, feel free to turn on the TV, explore, make yourself at home," Koa urged. He took a step toward her as if he were going to kiss her again and then halted. "Let me go shower."

"I'll be here," she answered, smiling at him. Giana enjoyed thinking that he liked kissing her. She definitely had enjoyed his attention.

He disappeared down the hall, and she heard water running. "Oh!" That wouldn't help her need to use the bathroom. Giana squeezed her legs together as the urge became an emergency. Maybe he had two bathrooms.

Koa had told her to explore. Giana bit her lip, trying to figure out what to do. She could jump in her truck and go to a public restroom. She looked around for a way to leave him a note. If only she could spot a notepad. She couldn't just disappear.

Giana didn't think she'd make it somewhere ten or even five minutes away. Standing, she walked down the hall, checking for another bathroom. She found a spare bedroom set up like a home gym and Koa's bedroom with its massive king-size bed. That made her stop for a minute as her imagination went wild.

The pressure of her bladder made her switch focus. There

wasn't another bathroom. Only the one he was currently naked inside.

Before she could stop herself, Giana knocked on the door. "Koa, I'm so sorry. I have to pee."

"Come in, little girl. I won't peek."

Giana didn't hesitate. She was used to sharing facilities with the other firefighters. Heck, she'd seen most of her colleagues naked and vice versa when they'd been exposed to dangerous chemicals while putting out a fire and had to strip off their clothes for decontamination. Giana pushed her pants down and collapsed onto the toilet. Knowing that he could hear her made this seem so intimate.

A soft hum came from behind the shower curtain, and then a smooth, low voice emerged. Koa was singing. His voice was amazing. Deep and rich, he added his own touch to the latest country hit Giana had heard on all the radio stations. The song covered any sound she made and soothed her jangled nerves.

Quickly, she finished and flushed the toilet, hoping it wouldn't affect the temperature in the shower. Giana washed her hands and squeaked a "thank you" before escaping out the door. His serenade followed her into the hall.

Giana leaned on the bathroom door, hugging herself. What a Daddy thing to do. How many men would have realized she was embarrassed and provided cover for her? More important than that, how many men wouldn't have peeked? In one move, Koa had proved to her he was truthful, reliable, and thoughtful.

She shook her head in amazement. How had she found him?

"Please let him be my daddy," she whispered.

"What? I'm sorry, I missed that," Koa said, opening the door. "Whoa!" He caught Giana as she fell inward to land against his chest.

"Oh! I'm sorry!" Giana said, trying to move away as soon as she'd regained her balance. She turned to face him to apologize one more time and swallowed her tongue.

Holy fuck! Did men have that many muscles? She stared at his body covered only by a towel wrapped around his waist. Her gaze dipped down past the delicious hip grooves to the damp material clinging to his pelvis. *OMG!*

"Fair warning, little girl. I'm going to pick you up and carry you to my bed in exactly five seconds if you don't backtrack to the couch."

Giana didn't move. She looked at his face in wonder. When he announced, "One," she took two steps forward to press herself against him. "Kiss me, Koa."

His deep growl did things to her inside. His arms tightened around her waist, hugging her to his hard muscles. Koa lowered his mouth to hers in what felt like slow motion, as if giving her time to change her mind. There was no way that was going to happen.

Giana rose on her tiptoes to speed up the process. She swept her tongue over the seam of his lips and slipped inside to taste him. Fresh mint signaled to her that he'd brushed his teeth. She missed his own flavor, but quickly pushed that aside as he deepened the kiss.

His hand trailed up her spine, making her shiver. Koa cupped the back of her head and held her in place as he took control of their exchange. His dominance made her feel sexier and freer. With him in charge, she simply needed to enjoy herself.

She wrapped her arms around his neck, clinging to him as he devoured her. Giana could feel herself responding to him. Her nipples tightened against Koa's hard chest, and she wiggled to brush them over his skin. She squeezed her thighs together as heat built between them, soaking her panties with her juices. She scooted her feet closer to press her pelvis to his hardening shaft.

Koa released her mouth. "Do you promise not to run away if I carry you into my bedroom?" he growled. "We can take this slow."

"I don't want to go slow. Make love to me, Koa."

"Daddy," he demanded.

Giana understood immediately. "Make love to me, Daddy."

Her world whirled around her as Koa lifted her to drape over his shoulder. She stared at the most perfectly formed male butt cheeks flexing as he carried her to his bed. His towel was crumpled and forgotten on the floor behind them.

"Come here, little girl," he said, lowering her feet to the floor. "You are way overdressed."

Giana grabbed the bottom of her shirt. She'd only lifted it a couple of inches before his hands stopped hers. She glanced up in surprise.

"Daddy gets to unwrap his present."

"Present?" she echoed.

"Best damn present I've ever received."

He tugged the shirt from her hands and whisked it over her head. After tossing it somewhere, Koa traced the delicate edge of her bra over the top of her breast. Giana bit her lower lip to prevent herself from moaning.

"Look how pretty you are. Daddy needs to take away this scratchy lace."

She nodded eagerly and held her breath as he traced the straps over her shoulders to the back fastener. Koa deftly released the hooks and smoothed the band from her skin. Giana shrugged her shoulders to help him, and the cups dropped away.

"You are so beautiful, little girl."

He tossed the scrap of lace away before cupping her

breasts. His thumbs brushed roughly over her sensitive skin. Giana closed her eyes to savor the sensation of his caresses. She blinked them open at the feel of his hot breath. To her delight, she watched Koa swirl his tongue over one budded peak before drawing it into the heat of his mouth. A moan of pleasure escaped her mouth, drawing his gaze to her.

"Mmm," he hummed on her skin, sending vibrations through her sensitive flesh.

Giana couldn't believe how everything felt better with him. It was as if he had a magic touch. "Please," she begged.

"I'm not going to rush this, little girl," he told her sternly before kissing a tantalizing path to her other breast and repeating his caresses.

When he released her nipple with an audible pop, Giana realized she wasn't returning his caresses. Afraid he would consider her a selfish lover, she lowered herself down onto her knees. Koa caught her and lifted her back to her feet.

"No, little girl. I'm not finished with you."

He unfastened her jeans and yanked the denim and her panties over her hips, throwing them to the floor. Kneeling on one leg, he scanned her curves slowly as Giana held her breath. He leaned forward to press his mouth to her mound before telling her, "You are an irresistible temptation. I need you in my bed now. Brace yourself on my shoulder and lift this foot." He tapped her left toes without glancing away.

Giana scrambled to follow his instructions and switched as soon as he finished with her shoe and clothing on one side. She tightened her fingers on his shoulder as he stood up, brushing his body against hers. Giana could feel the effect of her nakedness on him. Koa's thick, hot shaft pressed into her stomach.

He stroked her back and gripped her waist. "I need you, little girl. Do we need to discuss anything? I'm regularly tested on base to conform to regulations. I'm clean."

She blinked at him, struggling to focus on his words. "What?"

"I'm safe for you. Are you on birth control?"

Giana's face heated as she understood that time. Thankful he was thinking clearly to ask, she blurted, "I've been tested recently, too. I'm on the pill."

"Do you want me to wear a condom, Giana?" he asked, cupping her face. "I want to take care of you if that's what you prefer."

She swallowed hard and forced herself to be smart. "Maybe in the beginning?" she asked. If he fucked her and never pursued her again, she'd have one less thing to worry about. "I mean..."

"That's completely reasonable, Giana. Smart. I'm glad you take care of yourself, little girl. I'm going to earn your trust. I don't plan to go anywhere."

Her heart melted inside her chest. He made her feel so safe. "Make love to me, Koa. I need you."

His wolfish grin made her heart skip a beat. She'd never met anyone like him.

Koa swept her into his arms and laid her gently on the bed. Following her down to the mattress, he kissed and caressed her until Giana couldn't put a coherent thought together. She explored his hard angles, seeking to return the pleasure he lavished on her.

Koa trapped her wrists in his hands and yanked them over her head to pin her to the pillows. She stared up at him, panting with arousal. Had she done something wrong? "Koa?"

"I have to get the condom on, Flame. I need to calm down a minute or I'm going to come the moment I touch myself," he growled.

The corners of her lips twitched upward. Giana was ecstatic that she'd affected him so strongly. She playfully waggled her eyebrows at him, loving his honesty. Lifting her hips, she rubbed her pussy against his hard thigh.

"You are going to kill me, little girl." Koa kissed her hard before reaching for the drawer of his nightstand. He ripped open the small packet and rolled it onto his erection. When she licked her lips without thinking, he groaned and threatened, "I'm going to spank your bottom until it's fiery red, Flame."

When she nodded eagerly, he shook his head. "My cock is going to break off if you make me any harder. Damn. I need to be inside you now."

He pushed himself up to his hands and knees. Placing the head of his cock at her entrance, Koa pressed slowly inside. When she wrapped her legs around his waist and pulled him toward her faster, Koa pinned her hips to the mattress. "Slow, Giana. I don't want to hurt you."

As he filled her, her body stretched around him. The sensation combined pleasure and pain in an addictive rush that made her eyes roll up to the ceiling. "Eyes on me, Flame."

Her gaze fixed on his as he sank fully into her. Giana would never forget that intimate connection. She stared up into his face, suspecting she'd never be the same after his lovemaking.

"Are you okay, little girl?"

"Move, Koa. I need it all."

"That's my girl," Koa praised her and shared that wolfish grin that did funny things to her insides before slamming his mouth over hers in a punishing kiss that distracted her from his withdrawal. There was no way she missed his thrust back into her tight pussy.

She came harder than ever before, screaming into the room as she shattered. Giana gave up trying to remain in any semblance of control. She abandoned herself to the pleasure that Koa lavished on her.

When he came a long time later, she clung to his powerful body. Completely exhausted from the numerous climaxes he'd coaxed from her, Giana pressed kisses to every inch of skin she could reach. Thinking of her at all times, Koa moved to her side when their heart rates calmed. She clutched at him when Koa rolled toward the edge of the bed.

"Shh, little one. I'll be right back. I'm going to get rid of this condom."

When he returned, Koa brought a damp washcloth. He stroked it over her face and neck before using it to clean her juices from her thighs. Dropping the cloth next to the bed, Koa stretched out and pulled Giana close. He covered them with the sheet and kissed her temple.

"Nap, little girl. I'll fix us dinner in an hour."

Giana considered arguing, but being held in his arms was too delicious. She followed his directions and closed her eyes.

CHAPTER 5

For the first time ever, Koa regretted having to leave for work the next morning. He followed Giana's truck out of the neighborhood when she'd insisted on leaving with him. His only consoling memory as he watched her turn left while he headed to the right was that she'd programmed her address into his phone before kissing him goodbye. Today was going to creep past.

Heading into the base, he accepted the good-natured ribbing from the guards at the gate. The word of his special delivery had spread among those staffing the entrance. He shook his head and drove to his normal parking area. *Totally worth it.*

Once inside the large gathering area, Koa stowed his phone and keys in his locker. He'd just closed the metal door when a special tone rang from his device. Rolling his neck in disbelief at the crappy timing, he ripped the door open and grabbed his phone to read the message. Blindly finding his keys as he scanned the notice, Koa ran for his truck to grab a go-bag he always kept ready to go as he sent a message to Giana.

. . .

Flame,

My team has been activated. I don't know when I'll get back in town. You'll be my first phone call. I'll miss you.
Daddy

As he ran back inside, he found Jerico texting a message to Aspen and Zale disconnecting from a phone call. Both looked at him and understood immediately that Koa was in the same boat—having to notify his little girl.

Jerico walked forward and extended his hand. "The fire captain?" he asked. When Koa nodded, Jerico said, "Congratulations on finding your Little. Want Aspen to reach out to her if we're gone for a while?"

"Thanks." Koa thought about the second question for a minute. He didn't want to scare Giana. He didn't want her to panic if someone else knew she was little. His phone buzzed in his hand, displaying Giana's name.

"I'll ask her."

Koa stepped away. "Giana, I don't have much time. Do you want me to give your name and number to my team leader's little girl for her to contact you if we're gone for a while?"

"Koa, I don't want you to go."

"I know, little girl. My team and I are determined to finish the job we're sent on as fast as possible and get home safe. Would it help to have another little girl to talk to?" he asked.

"Is… Is she nice?"

"She's very sweet. You'll like Aspen. I'm sorry to rush you, Flame, but I have to get off the phone."

"Yes, give her my name and number," Giana said quickly. "Tell her I need this to be confidential."

"Aspen will guard your secrets," he promised without hesitation. "I'll see you soon, little girl. Take care of yourself."

"You, too, Daddy."

Koa disconnected and sent Jerico Giana's contact information. Jerico passed it along to Aspen with a message. Hanging his head, he allowed himself to lament the timing of this deployment. He'd just found her.

"Koa!" Caden called him from the doorway to the briefing room.

Fuck! Koa allowed himself to be pissed for a few seconds before forcing his brain into gear. Rule number one, don't let anything mess with your mind. That was a surefire way to get yourself and your team killed. He shrugged off his worries and headed to find out what they'd face.

* * *

THREE LONG WEEKS LATER, Koa walked back to his locker to grab his keys. The single members of the team joked and laughed, but Koa noticed he, Jerico, and Zale were quiet and focused. His only thought was to find Giana.

Walking out the door, he watched Aspen run to Jerico and Pippa smother Zale in a million kisses. His heart sank. No Giana.

"Jerico, I need to tell Koa something," Aspen said, stopping her daddy from carrying her away.

She ran to his side. "We couldn't get Giana on the base. She's waiting for you outside."

Koa's energy skyrocketed, and he raced for his truck. Risking the MPs fining him for speeding, he drove as quickly as possible through the gate.

"Welcome home, soldier," the guard called and pointed to the left.

Squinting into the late afternoon sun, Koa spotted her truck parked at the side of the road. He pulled behind her and jumped out of the cab. Gravel flew as he ran to her.

"Flame," he whispered, gathering her into his arms. "I missed you so much. Are you okay?"

"I'm good, Daddy. My heart is so happy to see you," Giana told him with tears in her eyes.

Koa pulled her against him and kissed her sweet lips. Instant heat swelled between them, pushing away the exhaustion from his mind. He forced himself to lift his mouth from hers. When she cupped his cheek with her hand, he turned his head to press a kiss to her palm.

"I'm sorry for the bad timing. Tomorrow, I'm getting you a base pass, little girl. I never want you to have to wait alone."

"Aspen and Pippa are awesome. They wanted to stay with me, but I sent them inside to greet their daddies and tell you where I was. I have Jellybean with me for protection," Giana explained, nodding at the stuffie sitting in the passenger seat.

"Hi, Jellybean. Aren't you pretty? I'm glad to see you're helping Giana. Thank you for keeping my little girl company," Koa told her.

Giana wrapped her arms back around his neck and hugged herself tighter to him. "I think the guards were concerned I was up to no good, but when I told them I was waiting for you, they were super nice."

Koa laughed. Those guards knew everyone's business. "They must have guessed you were the one who left a note for me with the day crew. Will you come home with me, Giana?"

"I'd love to, but my shift starts in an hour. I'm really glad you got home in time so I could see you. I'm so sorry I have to rush off."

He pulled back slightly to scan her. "I didn't even notice you were wearing your uniform. How long's your shift?"

"Twenty-four hours. Then I have some time off because I grabbed some extra shifts while you were gone. As the captain, I work with all the shifts on a rotation, so I see how everything is going with each crew."

"You have a lot of responsibility, Flame." He couldn't rip her clothes off here and show her how much he cared for her. Resigned to celebrating with her in twenty-five hours, he asked, "How did you get to be the captain so quickly?"

The guys had posed that question while they were deployed, and Koa hadn't known. That had earned him some ribbing about what they did other than talk when they were together. Good-natured teasing, of course. The team knew exactly how long he'd known Giana.

"A combination of knowledge, skills, and luck, I guess. I have a criminology degree. I did a stint as a parole officer, but it quickly became too dangerous," Giana admitted, shaking her head. "Unfortunately with the increasing violence endangering first responders of all kinds, my degree moved me up the chain of command in the fire department as a needed resource."

"And that's safer for you?"

"Definitely. I mean risks are everywhere, but I'm out with an entire team instead of meeting with dangerous individuals alone now."

"An excellent reason to make a switch, little girl. Were you hurt?" Koa kept his tone steady, despite his urge to take care of anyone who'd lifted a finger against her. Judging by her expression, there was more to the story than Giana simply taking a bit of time before starting a different career. Instantly, he was concerned about her safety, even if something had happened a few years ago.

"No, but several close calls. I lost my nerve, giving off the wrong vibe to bad guys. I had to make a change."

"I'm glad you did, Flame." Koa forced himself to relax. He didn't ask any more questions. His little girl was brave to face the truth head on.

She nodded and continued, "Anyway, I needed a break when I left criminal justice, so I went to my relative's farm to relax for a while. My grandfather had worked as a volunteer firefighter years ago. When I was sulking around, he set up an obstacle training course. To his complete surprise, I was a natural. He decided I must have inherited his side of the family's strength." Giana laughed and flexed her biceps.

"Being a firefighter has a huge physical component," Koa agreed. He'd very definitely noticed her toned muscles.

"He said my butt's big to store all my power," Giana shared with a laugh that contained a bit of self-consciousness.

"Funny, I thought your adorable butt was made for me to spank."

Her face blushed pink, and she dropped her forehead down to his shoulder. "That really turns me on," she admitted.

"A good girl spanking *should* turn you on. A bad girl spanking—not so much."

"I don't plan to be bad. I mean, I know there are Littles who brat. Aspen and Pippa admitted they sometimes deliberately do the wrong thing. I can't see myself doing that."

"A spanking can be a release if you're stressed or upset. Crying effectively releases all those pent-up feelings. Can you tell me if you need some extra discipline?" Koa asked, leaning back to scan her face.

Giana pressed her nose to his shirt and shook her head.

"Daddy needs to see you, Flame. I want to make sure you're okay," Koa said sternly. He cupped her cheeks and tilted her beautiful face up. She chewed on her bottom lip. Koa guessed she was fretting about his answer.

"This is a tough conversation to have in a few minutes. Would you feel better if I tell you I will give you whatever you need: a spanking, a hug, tender lovemaking, urgent sex, time as a very little Little. We'll experiment with everything and see what works for us."

Giana's breath gusted from her lungs. Her features softened as the tension drained from her expression. "I would enjoy experimenting and knowing that I don't have to do it again if I don't like it. Or you don't enjoy it," she added quickly.

"I'll be honest. I have some hard limits. How about if I send you a list of activities anyone might explore in a BDSM relationship, and you can check it out if you have free time and privacy at work?"

"Hard limits mean those things you don't want to do?" she asked.

When he nodded, Giana hesitated. Helping her, he clarified, "I'm not a fan of knife or blood play, strap-ons, and humiliation. Can you live without those?"

"Oh, I wouldn't like those either," she agreed with a shudder.

"There may be some others you'd like to take off. Be honest. Daddy will pick up if you lie about something you don't want because you think I am into it," Koa warned.

A honk drew their attention as Aspen and Jerico drove past followed by Pippa, Zale, and the rest of the team heading home. Koa loved Giana's enthusiastic waves at her new friends. He loved that she'd already bonded with the other little girls.

Koa tightened his arms around her waist and kissed her soundly. "I've missed holding you as I sleep, little girl."

"We only shared a bed once," she said.

"We did. Somehow, the amount of time wasn't important. My heart has already decided you're mine. I don't plan to let you go, Flame."

"Do you call me Flame because I'm a firefighter?"

"No, Giana. Because I'm drawn to you like a moth to a flame. You're irresistible," Koa told her.

They both looked down at her arm when a beep sounded.

"Oh, no. I have to go, Koa. I'm so sorry."

"Call me Daddy and I'll forgive you," he told her before pressing a soft kiss to her irresistible lips.

"I'm so glad you're home, Daddy," she whispered.

"Will you come to my house when you get off?" he asked. "We have three days off before our training starts again."

"In less than twenty-five hours, I'll pound on your door," she promised.

"I'm going to hold you to that." Koa stepped back and helped Giana into her truck. He didn't move from that spot until she had disappeared from sight. Then, he dragged himself back to his vehicle and climbed inside. He'd go get some sleep to revitalize while he waited for her.

CHAPTER 6

Giana spotted Koa from several houses away and barely kept herself from drooling. Her buff daddy wore only a brief pair of training shorts as he pushed the mower around the yard. It looked like he'd already cut his neighbors' lawns on each side of him and only had a small patch left to go. She slowed to watch the amazing scenery as his toned body maneuvered the rumbling machine across the grass.

When he turned to mow that final strip, Koa noticed her. He ran the mower forward, finishing the job as she pulled into his driveway. She'd barely gotten the truck turned off when he reached her. Giana threw open the door and tumbled out into his arms, confident he would catch her.

"I'm so sorry. I couldn't believe it when that jerk ran into the firetruck on our last call. The paperwork is always a bear."

"You're here now. That's all that matters," Koa told her and kissed her hard. "Come inside. I'll shower. I'm not always this sweaty."

"I have to grab Jelly."

"Of course." Koa opened the passenger door and retrieved the plain canvas bag. The bunny stuffie disguised herself inside when Giana took her on an excursion.

"You are great eye candy for the housewives around you," she teased as they walked up to the door.

"All the housewives around here have their own husbands to entertain them, little girl. They were glad I was here to repay their favor of mowing my lawn while I was gone."

"Your neighbors mowed for you?" she asked in surprise. She hadn't considered that he'd need someone to take care of that for him.

"We watch out for each other here in off-base housing. I'll do the same for them if their soldier is deployed and I'm here. Are you hungry, little girl?"

"Only for you," she dared to say as he opened the door.

Koa wrapped one arm around her and lifted Giana from her feet. He set Jelly in her arms.

"Whoa!" she yelped as he carried her inside and slammed the door shut behind them. He balanced her in his arms as he stepped out of his work sneakers. With that done, he carried her purposefully toward his master bathroom and set her feet on the tile in the center of the room.

"Let's set Jelly on the dresser," he suggested. When she nodded her agreement, he took the bag and placed it safely out of the way.

"No peeking, Jelly," he told the stuffie. He turned to focus on Giana as she giggled.

"Undo those buttons," he ordered, pointing to her pressed, collared shirt. "Unless you want me to rip them off?"

Koa dropped to his knees in front of her and unfastened her pants. He yanked them to her ankles before unlacing her boots. "Step," he ordered, and when she lifted one foot he shucked off her footwear and clothing before repeating the action for her other side.

"You're bossy," she observed as she shrugged out of her shirt.

"You're slow," he answered, focusing on the cleavage she revealed as she tossed away the garment.

"You're still dressed," she reminded him as she grabbed the band of the exercise bra she always wore to work and tugged it over her head.

The heat already brewing in his gaze had skyrocketed like the fire from the wings that introduced them when their gaze met again. Inside, Giana did a happy dance seeing his attraction to her. Outwardly, she maintained a straight face as she pointed to his tented shorts.

"Don't you want to take those off?" Giana suggested.

With a growl of impatience, Koa stripped off the sweaty garment and tossed it over his shoulder. Purposefully herding her into the oversized walk-in shower stall, Koa turned on the water and adjusted it, keeping her safe from the spray until he was satisfied. He stepped under the showerhead and let the water cascade over him before reaching out a blind hand to find her and gently tug her forward into his arms.

Closing her eyes as the warm liquid streamed over her, Giana responded eagerly to Koa's scorching kiss. He held her close. His skin radiated heat from the sun. Giana pressed herself against him, loving how his hard angles fit perfectly to hers.

When he lifted his head to allow her to breathe, she shook the water from her face and met his gaze. "Make love to me, Koa. I need you."

His quick inhale warned her to fill her lungs. His mouth captured hers in a hard kiss that demanded everything from her. Giana returned it with the same intensity. The firehouse was torture last night. Her mind had replayed the pleasure Koa had shared with her during their night together. Fearing she would talk in her sleep, she had tossed and turned all night.

Koa released her lips and lowered himself to his knees, pressing her to the side of the shower. His tongue licked a path down her abdomen to her sensitive mound. When he pulled gently at her trimmed adult curls, Giana gasped at the slight taste of pain and celebrated that she'd decided not to have a full Brazilian wax. Her juices practically squirted from her as he gripped her hips, pressing her to the chilly tiles. She suspected his fingers would leave marks and loved his urgency.

When he lifted one of her legs over his shoulder, Giana wobbled for a second as she regained her balance. His hands held her securely as his gaze focused directly on her pussy. Koa inhaled deeply. The animalistic move fueled her desire. Hunger etched itself onto his features as he met her gaze.

"I'll never get enough of you, little girl," he told her. His gravelly deep voice dispelled all the butterflies in her stomach. Nothing else mattered except for her and him.

Koa lowered his mouth to her mound. He devoured her with enthusiasm and skill that caused her eyes to roll up in her head. When everything stopped, she focused back on his face.

"Eyes on me, Giana. Don't look away."

She nodded, ready to agree to anything he'd demand. Giana needed him to continue.

"Good girl," he praised her.

His words pushed her arousal higher. Suddenly, she wanted to be good for him more than anything else in the world. Watching him tease and taste her was the hottest thing she'd ever experienced. His lips glistened with her juices as his tongue intimately explored her. When he pressed two fingers deep into her, all the swirling sensations exploded, and with a keening cry, she climaxed, wobbling on her suddenly unsteady leg.

Releasing her leg, Koa stood to wrap his arm around her waist. He held her pressed to the tile as he caressed her, pushing her pleasure higher than she'd ever imagined. Captured by his gaze trapping her, Giana reached out to caress him. She wrapped her fingers around his thick shaft and squeezed.

"Damn, that feels amazing, Flame. I'm going to stretch this tight pussy with my cock as soon as you come again."

She nodded eagerly, wanting everything he promised. She could feel the orgasm he promised hovering close. If only she could grab it.

"Come, little girl," he ordered and pinched her clit.

Giana screamed as her climax crashed over her, shaking her. She clung to his strength as Koa lifted her, holding her tight to his torso as he carried her out of the shower.

"I've got to grab a condom, Flame."

"Nothing between us, Daddy. I'm protected."

He didn't hesitate, but boosted her higher on the tiles. Automatically, she wrapped her thighs around his waist as he fitted himself to her. As her body still spasmed with aftershocks, he thrust firmly into her. Still, his gaze held her captive. Skin to skin, he filled her completely.

Forging a miles-deep connection between them as he powered into her, Koa's deep eyes seemed to see into her soul. Giana didn't want this to end. Her hands glided over his wet skin as she memorized his incredible form.

The faint splatter of the water turned cold, but nothing distracted him. Giana came over and over. When Koa finally allowed himself to climax, she smoothed her hands over his chest and shoulders as he shook with the intensity of the sexual thrill that he'd lavished on her.

Koa held her close until he recovered. Then he washed

them both as she struggled to stand. After wrapping her in a soft towel, her daddy carried her to his bed. He dried her gently and laid her on the soft sheets. Within seconds, he curled himself around her and drew the covers up to keep her warm.

"I'm so glad you're home, Daddy," Giana mumbled and felt his kiss on her temple. She heard the rumble of his deep voice, but didn't grasp the words as sleep claimed her.

CHAPTER 7

Waking up immediately as his little girl rolled toward the edge of the bed, Koa asked, "You okay, Flame?"

"Just running to the bathroom," she explained. He could hear the faint embarrassment in her tone.

"That's allowed," he teased and was pleased to see the tension in her shoulders ease. "Need help?"

"No, Daddy," she said and fled for the bathroom with pink cheeks.

After checking the clock to see it was slightly past seven in the evening, Koa swung his feet over the side and stood. As he made his bed, Koa fluffed the pillow on Giana's side. A whiff of her scent tantalized him. He pressed his face into the stuffing and inhaled.

"You're not smothering yourself, are you?" she asked with an arched eyebrow.

Koa dropped the pillow back to the bed and walked toward her. "I'll get my fix from the original source." He buried his head in the crook of her neck and sniffed.

"You're smelling me?" she asked, laughing.

"A long-lasting holdover from our caveman days. I've imprinted on your scent," he explained in mock educationalese.

"Caveman days? I'll believe that! Got a T-shirt or something I can wear? You're going to tire of me parading around nude," she said.

Koa placed his hand on her forehead as if checking for a fever. "Maybe I should grab my thermometer. You must be coming down with something if that idea even pops into your mind."

Playing along, she opened her mouth as if waiting for the instrument.

Koa gently lifted her lower jaw to shut her mouth. "That's not where little girls have their temperature taken," he told her and patted her cute bottom.

The play of emotions on her face was adorable. Shock. Disbelief. Interest. Arousal. She was such a precious little girl. He waited patiently.

"I feel wonderful—not sick at all," she assured him.

"I'm glad." Koa walked over to his dresser and grabbed a T-shirt and shorts. She could pull the string tight, and they'd probably stay up. If they didn't… well, he could live with that. "Let's see if you'll be comfortable in these. I'll clear out a drawer for you."

"Do you think that's moving too fast? My bringing clothes over here?" she asked, worrying her bottom lip with her teeth.

"It doesn't seem fast to me. I'd move you in permanently tomorrow. What's more important is how you feel. Is it too early in our relationship for you?" Koa asked.

Giana stared at him for a few seconds and slowly shook her head. "I'm baffled why I feel so confident about this, but no. I enjoy being with you. I missed you so much while you were gone."

Koa walked forward and pulled her into his arms. He hugged her tightly before dropping a kiss on the top of her head. When he heard her exhale strongly, he cupped her jaw to tilt her gaze up to meet his. "I missed you too, Flame. How about if we spend time together and not worry about whether it's the conventional thing to do? No one gets any say in what we do except us."

She nodded immediately. "I'd like that." Her stomach growled loudly.

"Then that's what we do. First, we get you dressed, and then I get us some food."

"I don't need anything fancy," she told him. "A sandwich is great… Or something frozen."

"You'll get Daddy's fancy, make-ahead taco feast." Koa stepped back and grabbed the shirt, pulling it over her head.

"Daddy's fancy, make-ahead taco feast?" The fabric muffled her voice.

Koa smiled and tugged the opening over her head. "Exactly. I took advantage of downtime to get everything together so that when you got here, we could concentrate on other things."

"Do you have groceries here? We could go out," she suggested.

"I'm not ready to share you with the world, little girl," he told her honestly and watched her smile at that thought.

"Possessive much?"

"Definitely."

"I like tacos," she offered a subject change.

"The world of taco fans is filled with controversy. Are you team soft or hard taco?"

She studied his face before commenting, "I'm picking up that there's a right and a wrong answer to your question."

"Definitely."

Giana sighed and answered, "Hard. Soft tortillas get mushy."

Koa lifted her into his arms and whirled her around the room to celebrate her correct opinion. "I knew you were the perfect little girl for me." He kissed her deeply and couldn't resist stealing a few more smooches before setting her physically away from him.

"Let's get you all covered up before I toss you back on the bed," Koa told her as he picked up the shorts he'd grabbed for her to wear.

In a couple of minutes, he led her to the kitchen and pulled out one of the high-backed stools at the island. "Sit and tell me what you were up to while I was gone."

"I can help."

"Not going to happen. Daddy takes care of the kitchen. Too many hot and pokey things for little girls. How many shifts did you pick up?"

He stood holding the chair for her until Giana climbed up on the stool. "Thank you, Flame." He kissed her head before scooting her to the counter.

"I don't want to take advantage of you."

"That won't happen." Koa grabbed a package of animal crackers and opened it to scatter a few on the island before her. Giana picked up one to figure out which animal it was and then bit its head off.

Bloodthirsty. I love it.

"I did my regular shifts the first week, and then when I didn't hear from you, I filled in my schedule."

"Like every day?"

Koa opened the refrigerator and pulled out a bunch of different-sized containers. He carried them to the table and popped open the tops to reveal all the best taco fixings: shredded lettuce, cheddar cheese, tomatoes, jalapenos, salsa, pineapple, and diced ham.

I wonder how adventurous my little girl is with food?

"Yeah. Being at my apartment was lonely and boring. I didn't want to go out and do stuff," she admitted, shrugging her shoulders. "Is that SPAM?"

"Yes, have you ever tried it on a taco?" He reached back into the fridge to pull out the ground beef he'd already browned.

"Never. And is that pineapple?"

"Yes. They go together very well," he told her as he vented the lid of the seasoned hamburger and put it in the microwave to heat. "No worries, I have regular taco meat as well."

Opening the pantry, he found the package of hard taco shells and loaded them into the air fryer as he concentrated on his little girl.

Giana picked up another animal cookie and bit off the animal's legs first this time. She really was a bloodthirsty muncher, he thought, controlling the smile that threatened. Koa didn't want her to think he was making fun of her.

"Would you make me a taco the way you like them? I want to try it."

"Of course." Koa pulled out a large gallon jug of milk and poured two glasses.

"No milk for me, please."

"Little girls need milk to grow strong and happy."

"Milk won't make me happy," she told him.

"Are you allergic to milk?" He watched her carefully, ignoring the beeping microwave behind him.

"Well… no. But I don't like it."

"Thank you for being honest." Koa carried the two glasses to the table.

Giana stiffened on the stool and pinned him with a look that probably scared her underlings at the fire station. "You're going to make me drink it?"

"I'm going to make you try it. If you want something different after drinking half of the glass, we'll talk." He grabbed potholders and removed the covered dish from the microwave.

"You're not the boss of me," she snapped.

"Are you sure about that? I think having a daddy implies that he's in charge." Koa set the dish on a potholder on the table and returned to grab the crisp taco shells, two plates, napkins, and silverware.

She stared at him as he bustled around, struggling to find fault with his logic. Finally, she said, "But being in charge doesn't mean being a bully."

"Definitely not. As a little girl, you can always use your safeword to stop. Come join me at the table," he said and pulled a chair out for her.

"I don't have a safeword." Giana picked up her last animal cracker and slid off the stool to walk over and sit down. She carefully placed the small giraffe-shaped treat next to her.

"What would you like to use? Something preferably that you wouldn't say normally," Koa suggested as he slid her closer to the table. "Red is easy to start with."

"That works," she said, shrugging. "I won't ever use it."

"Yes, you will. If you need to, I'm trusting you to tell me when something is too much. Little girls have an extremely important job. Much more important than a daddy's," Koa told her as he picked up a shell and put together a delicious concoction for Giana.

"How do you figure that?" she asked.

"For me, being a daddy is taking care of someone in a very intimate way. I'm trying to figure out what you want and need in every interaction. What if I read your expression wrong? Or your desires for that day at that moment? It can either cause an enormous problem, maybe the end of a relationship, or you can clue a clueless daddy in. Which sounds better? Me blindly guessing or me pushing your boundaries and knowing you'll let me know before I pass the point you'll want me as your daddy? Here. Try this, Flame."

He set the taco on her plate. Koa could almost hear the wheels churning in her mind as she considered his words. Slowly, she picked up the taco and took a bite.

"Mmm!" she hummed as she wiggled in her chair. "That's amazing!"

"I'm glad you like it. Want me to make you another?"

"More jalapenos," she requested.

"One more. I don't want to set your mouth on fire and have to call the fire department," he teased as he created another masterpiece.

"I love ham and pineapple as a topping. It adds so much flavor with the spices."

"Trying new things can be scary, but sometimes there are huge rewards for stepping out of your comfort zone," he said, setting the second taco on her plate. He didn't link the two conversations together, but hoped she'd automatically make the connection.

"You've already figured out I have a slight control problem, haven't you?" she asked, staring at him as he put another taco together.

"Perhaps. It's also human nature to resist new things, even if you know deep inside what you crave."

Giana took a big drink of milk and pulled back the glass to consider the beverage. Koa took a bite of his taco. Would she refuse to drink it? To his delight, she set it down and picked up her other taco without a word.

"Was it scary on your mission?" she asked.

Even though her tone was light, he could tell she'd worried about him. "There were some challenging moments, but Caden works our butts off to make sure we were ready. Besides, I know my team has my back."

"You like them a lot."

"They're my battle brothers. That's a stronger bond than most siblings have," he tried to explain.

"Aspen and Pippa love their daddies so much. I enjoyed getting to know Jerico and Zale through them. They had some good stories about the team."

"Of course they did. What did they tell you about me?" Koa asked, preparing himself to hear the worst.

"They think you'll be an amazing daddy."

"And…" Koa waited for the bad stuff.

"That's it. We talked about everyone's tattoos. They think you have the most."

"Probably. Tribal tattoos are very common in Hawaii." Koa made a few more tacos as they talked. From the way she inhaled them, he suspected Giana hadn't eaten well while he was gone.

"I've never been to Hawaii."

"We'll go sometime. Fair warning, I have an enormous family. We love to hang out together at someone's house, the beach, anywhere."

"That's fun. I have a few relatives I'm close to. My grandfather, most of all. He's the best," Giana shared.

"I'd love to meet him. Does he live in town?"

"About an hour away." She hesitated for a second before adding, "You're planning on us meeting each other's families?"

"Flame, I want it all—us living together, spending time with family, hanging with my team and the other Littles. Does that scare you?"

She shook her head. "It sounds incredible." Giana drained the last of her milk and asked, "Can I have more?"

"You bet, baby girl." Koa got up and grabbed the jug from the refrigerator and filled both their glasses without commenting on her change of attitude.

"Tell me something funny that happened to you all. I want to know it's not all danger all the time."

"Zale got bitten by a leech on his balls. He's our medic. He usually deals with all that. We had to play rock, paper, scissors to choose who pulled it off for him."

"Really?" Giana asked with a shudder. "I'd be out of there if something were sucking my blood."

"No, it really didn't happen like that. Hank was the closest. He took care of it with one eye closed."

"Why did he close one eye?"

"He's our sniper." Koa pantomimed arming a sniper rifle and closed his left eye as he focused through the pretend scope. "He always does that when he concentrates. It's ingrained in him. Watch the next time we're all together. You'll see it."

"You're very observant, aren't you?"

"I try to be. Want another taco?" he asked, waving at almost empty containers.

"No way. I can't believe I ate that many."

"You were hungry. Want to choose a movie while I toss these dishes into the dishwasher? After our nap, we may not get sleepy for a while."

"I can help."

"Never going to happen. Daddy's job. Take your giraffe cracker over to the couch and munch on it for dessert as you master the remote."

"Um, I think I'll run home and pick up a few things."

"I'll drive you. Can you wait for a few minutes?" Koa asked.

"Oh, I can be there and back before you finish."

"Let's take a few minutes at your place to grab some clothes for a few days. We'll need your other stuffie, too."

Her eyes widened as her jaw dropped. Pulling herself

together, Giana asked, "How do you know I have another stuffie?"

"You talked in your sleep earlier. By the third time you whispered Tiger, I'd eliminated another boyfriend and figured he was your stuffie, too."

"Oh!" she said and looked down at the table. "Do you think I'm silly?"

"Let's see. We've already established that you're a little girl, and that I want to be your daddy. Why would you think having two stuffies would make you silly? Unless that other stuffie is a giraffe named Tiger?" he guessed, teasing her.

Giana's gaze flew up to meet his as her mouth rounded in an astonished O. "How did you know?"

"That one cracker is precious to you. Elephants, horses, lions met a munchy death at your hands—legs, heads, butts chewed off without a care. The giraffe you couldn't eat. And a giraffe is the same colors as a tiger. It makes perfect sense."

"Of course it does!" blasted from her lips as she raised her arms in a victory sign. "Why can no one else understand that?"

She lowered her hands to the table as she stared at him. "You do though, don't you? You understand me."

"I hope so, little girl. If I miss something, you'll clue me in, won't you? Even daddies need some help sometimes. Now, give me five minutes and we'll go get Tiger."

"And some underwear," she quickly added.

"Whatever you want to bring," he assured her and stood. Koa dropped a kiss on the top of her head. Thank goodness he'd ordered those animal crackers.

CHAPTER 8

The complex was quiet when they pulled into the parking lot. Koa parked his car in her spot. Light still shone from a couple of windows, but most were dark. He scanned the area as they walked to the building. Neatly trimmed bushes and trees sat away from the locked entrance.

Giana grabbed her mail from her box in the small lobby before leading him up the stairs to her third-floor apartment. He took her keys to open the door and deadbolt. So far, he was pleased with her choice of living space. Koa ushered his little girl inside. Her apartment had revealed a lot. Sparsely decorated, the living room area looked like anyone could live there.

"How long have you lived here, Flame?"

"About five years. I'll go grab a bag and Tiger."

"I'll come with you."

"No. I mean, that's not necessary. I'll just be a couple of minutes. Could you check the fridge for anything that will go bad in a few days?" Giana requested, obviously coming up with something to occupy him.

"Of course." Koa headed for the small kitchen. Opening

the refrigerator, he stared at the glare of the light on the empty shelves. One lone withered apple sat in a bin. Shaking his head, he closed the door.

He walked down the hall to her bedroom. Koa scanned the room in amazement. Here was where his little girl lived. Her queen-size bed had a pink upholstered headboard in the shape of a crown, complete with jewels at the elevated points. Giana crammed clothes into a suitcase open on the mattress, obviously rushing.

"Let's fold those clothes, little girl," he suggested, walking forward.

"Oh! You can wait for me out there."

"Not happening." Koa pulled a wad of clothes out of the suitcase and selected a pair of jeans to straighten.

"I can get these. I didn't want to delay you," Giana said quickly, grabbing the jeans from his hands.

"I'm a competent packer, Giana. What are you afraid of?" he asked.

"Um, I'm not afraid of anything. It's just these are my private things—my private space."

"I don't think there are many secrets between us now, little girl. What's going on?"

Her mouth opened and closed several times. Finally, she whispered, "I don't know."

Koa stepped closer and pulled her into his arms. He held her close, rubbing her back. Under his hands, he could feel her heart beating quickly. "You're safe with me, Flame. I would rather cut off my own arm than hurt you. Take a deep breath with me," Koa instructed. He inhaled audibly and felt her follow his lead.

"Now, exhale. That's my good girl. Let's try it again."

On their third breath together, tension ebbed from her muscles. "That's better. Should we take Tiger and go? We can come back another day."

"No," she said, shaking her head and clutching him tighter.

"You know I'll hold you as long as you need my arms around you, Flame. Are you scared of something?"

She nodded, hiding her face in his chest.

"Talk to Daddy, little girl. What are you afraid of?"

"No one's ever seen this side of me. What if you decide I'm too much or too much work? I mean… Look at this room. It's way over the top."

"And you love every minute you spend in here, don't you?"

Giana peeked up at him and nodded.

Damn, she's the cutest. The impact she had already on his heart rocked him. Koa cupped her jaw and lowered his lips to hers. He kept the kiss sweet and reassuring. She relaxed against him.

When he lifted his mouth from hers, Koa captured her gaze with his. "I want to see all of you—the little side and the sassy adult side. You're safe with me, Giana. I'm going to prove that to you, but for now, will you trust me?"

"Yes, Daddy," she whispered.

"Thank goodness, because I really want to know where you got that," he asked, pointing to the remote lying next to her bed. A plastic shell surrounded the traditional black device, transforming it into a magic wand. Whoever had designed that was a genius. And Koa bet either a daddy or a Little.

"On the internet. It's over the top, isn't it?"

"No way. I want one for my house. We'll search for it tomorrow and order one." He squeezed her and winked. "I can't wait to discover all the magic you'll bring to my life."

"Can we take my headboard?" she asked.

"Let's move any furniture you want tomorrow so we

don't wake up the neighbors. Can you sleep one night in my boring bed?"

"It's not boring." Her face turned a delightful shade of pink.

"Definitely not with my cute little girl in it. What do you say? Shall we pack a few things and take Tiger home?" Koa suggested.

"Yes, please."

He kissed her lightly before stepping back to pick up the jeans and fold them. When Giana joined him, Koa glanced around the room. He couldn't spot Tiger anywhere.

"Tiger's not going to stampede over me, is he?"

Giggles filled the air, making him smile. "No, Daddy. Tiger is stealthy, though. He hides under my covers because he catches neck colds easily."

"A neck cold, hmmm?" Koa couldn't wait to see this stuffie. "Would you introduce us?"

Giana leaned over the bed, showcasing her sweet ass. Koa grabbed a pair of shorts and folded them to keep his hands busy. He'd squeeze that delectable derriere later.

"Here he is," Giana announced, pulling a foot-tall giraffe stuffie out from under the bedspread. She held him to her chest with one hand as she levered herself up with the other. Koa dropped the material in his hands to lift her back to her feet.

"Thanks, Daddy. This is Tiger."

"Hello, Tiger. I am very pleased to meet you." Koa could see from the worn plush how much Giana loved her stuffie. She'd dressed the giraffe in what appeared to be a red knee-high sock that stretched from under his chin to his shoulders.

"Red is Tiger's and my favorite color," she said.

"Tiger looks perfectly dashing in crimson."

"Do you like red, Daddy?"

"I do like red. I spend a lot more time wearing green or tan camouflage."

"Maybe they make red camouflage?"

"They should. Tiger, would you like to come visit my house? Maybe stay for a while?" Koa asked.

Giana bent her head to confer with her stuffie. After a brief pause, she asked, "Can we free all the giraffe animal crackers from the box they're in?"

"What would Tiger like to do with them?" Koa asked.

"He would like to take them to the zoo to visit their relatives."

"Of course. We can do that."

"Perfect. He's excited to come with me now," Giana admitted.

"I'm glad. Shall we get these clothes packed? Is there anything else you'd like to take with you?"

"We have to get Tiger's suitcase, too. It's on the dresser."

Koa turned and spotted a good-sized satchel on the dresser. It had an official tag that announced the name Tiger. "I see that. It will definitely need to come with us."

He scanned the items in her suitcase. "I see jeans, shorts, T-shirts… What about panties? Work clothes? Do you have a nightie and slippers?"

She scurried around the room, adding more things to her suitcase as he folded the items in the original pile. Giana hesitated next to one nightstand. "Can I bring my reader?"

"Of course. We can read together sometimes. I have several on my tablet I wish to read."

"You don't read aloud, do you?"

"I do. Do you like listening to stories?"

She nodded and pulled open the drawer just enough to slide her hand inside. Something rattled inside, and then a very distinctive hum sounded. She fumbled around in the drawer desperately trying to silence that noise. Finally, she yanked it open and grabbed the vibrator to switch it off.

"Shall we take your toy as well?" Koa suggested, loving the red blush that colored her cheeks and throat.

"Daddy!"

"Daddies like to play with toys as well, little girl." He set down the T-shirt he held and walked around the bed to hold out his hand. "Maybe I'll like yours."

She hid the toy behind her back. "It's… It's broken now. I broke it."

He didn't answer, but moved his hand closer to her. Koa held her gaze. "Hand it to Daddy."

Ever so slowly, Giana drew her hand back in front of her body. She hesitated and then placed the wand vibrator in his hand.

"Thank you, Flame." Koa sat on the side of the bed and set it next to his thigh. "Now, let's deal with your lie."

"I didn't lie."

"If I check it, your toy won't hum?"

"Well, maybe now. It… It overheats and stops working."

"I don't think I believe you. Want to try another excuse?"

She shook her head slowly.

"Come here, Giana." Koa guided her faltering steps until she stood between his legs. "You've earned your first spanking. I will never allow lies to separate us."

"I didn't know that was a rule," she protested.

"I never mentioned that it was a rule. Perhaps you suspected lying to a daddy was a bad thing to do?"

Giana hesitated and nodded. "All the little girls and boys in my books get spanked when they lie."

"Sounds like your bottom needs to learn the lesson your brain already had memorized."

Koa didn't wait for her to answer or protest. He simply unfolded the top of her borrowed shorts and untied the string holding them in place. With a gentle push over her hips from Koa, the borrowed garment tumbled to the floor. Giana moved her hands to shield her mound.

"No hiding from Daddy. Move your hands to your sides, please."

He waited for her to choose to obey. After a second, she slowly followed his directions. "Good girl." Koa ruffled the silky hair that guarded her cleft. "Perhaps you would feel littler if we removed this."

She shivered in front of him. He could see how hard she was trying to be brave. Koa threaded his fingers through her thick brown hair and tugged slightly, drawing a moan of arousal from her lips. "Stop thinking from here, little girl, and," Koa leaned forward to press his lips between her breasts over her heart, "feel from here."

When he leaned back to check her reaction, Giana nodded. Her shoulders dropped away from her ears.

"Good girl," he praised her. "It's time to stretch out over my lap. I'll help you."

Giana closed her eyes, but allowed him to move her into position on his thighs. She clung to his calf. Her fingernails were already biting slightly into his skin.

Koa could feel his cock hardening in his jeans as he rubbed his hand over her buttocks and enjoyed the feel of her soft skin under his palm. He raised his hand and popped her lightly. His little girl jumped at the sensation. He didn't wait, but continued to pepper light swats across her buttocks and upper thighs as he assessed her pain tolerance.

She's more startled than hurt.

His shaft now pressed urgently against the metal zipper of his jeans. Koa flipped open the button securing his waistband, easing the tension a bit before increasing the strength of his punishment. Giana shifted restlessly on his lap, trying to avoid his hand. Koa tethered her in place with his free hand and enjoyed the view of her squirming body. *She is so beautiful.*

Her activity told him he needed to push her a bit further. The next spank that landed on her bottom left a red handprint on her now pink skin. Giana froze and then thrashed her legs. Koa quickly captured her kicking limbs with his leg, controlling her movements as he continued to smack her butt.

"Stop, Daddy!" Giana pleaded, looking back at him.

"You're taking your spanking well, Flame. Remember, you have a safeword. Use it if you need it."

"Can't it be done?"

"Not yet, little girl. Daddy knows when to stop. Tell me. What did you do to earn a spanking?" Koa wanted her to think about her actions. She needed to learn from this.

"I… I lied," she admitted.

"Lying isn't good for a relationship, is it, Giana?"

"Noooo!" she wailed.

He watched the tension vanish from her body as she submitted fully. Koa treasured her littleness. *I am so lucky to have found her.*

She rested heavily on his thighs, not moving, allowing him to punish her as he wished. Finally, she released her stranglehold on her emotions. Her quiet sobs reached him.

"I'm sorry, Daddy. I won't lie again."

Switching from spanking to rubbing, Koa smoothed his hand over her red skin. He allowed her to cry for a few seconds, to surrender fully before scooping her up in his arms and setting her bottom on his hard thigh. Her heat radiated through his jeans.

"Ouch, Daddy." Giana hid her face against his chest as he rocked her slowly in his arms.

Treasuring this delectable handful, Koa couldn't believe

the strength of his emotions for her. He would never let her go.

"A spanking doesn't teach a little girl a lesson if she doesn't feel it. Your red bottom will remind you for a bit how important it is to tell Daddy the truth."

"I'm never going to lie ever," she promised.

"You will, and your bottom will pay the consequence. Or Daddy will punish you in a different way."

"How?" she asked, peeking up at him. Her beautiful face was blotchy, but not drawn with discomfort or pain.

"Daddy might put a plug in your bottom. Or stand you in the corner after writing lines. Or I could use all three in succession. You could earn other punishments as well."

"I don't want any of those."

"Of course not. Punishment isn't meant to be fun." He cupped her bottom and squeezed, reminding Giana of the heat.

"Little girls can earn some rewards as well. Spread your legs for me, Flame."

She hesitated and squeezed her thigh muscles together. "No, Daddy."

"Should I turn you back over? Maybe I stopped your spanking too early."

"Daddy!" Giana shook her head quickly.

Giana swallowed hard and then inched her knees apart. "More, little girl. Daddy needs to see how your spanking affected you."

Slowly, she widened her legs, giving him lots of time to stop her. Koa didn't. He said nothing until she parted her legs as much as possible on his lap. "That's my good girl. Stay like that while Daddy checks to see if the spanking helped you."

Starting at her hips, he stroked his hands down to her inner thighs. His fingers dipped into her wetness. Her juices thoroughly coated her pussy. His cock jerked eagerly in his pants, and Koa clamped down on his control.

"So responsive. I am a very lucky daddy."

He stroked her pink folds until Giana moved toward his fingers, seeking more contact. Koa caressed her until her muscles tensed. Stopping his intimate caresses, he shifted his hand to ruffle her silky adult hair.

"Daddy, please."

"Not yet, Flame. Daddy needs to help you remember to be little."

"You want me to shave? I did go get waxed."

"No, sweetheart. Little girls don't play with razors. Daddy will take care of this for you." Koa stood, lifting her to stand on her feet. "Let's go to your bathroom."

Giana turned to look back at him. Heat shone in his eyes, revealing his arousal. She scanned his body and stared at his burgeoning shaft. She lifted a hand toward him.

"No, Giana. You don't have permission to touch Daddy now. Bathroom, little girl."

Nodding, she dropped her hand and scurried to the bathroom. Koa picked up Tiger and the vibrator. She might need the reassurance of her stuffie. Holding her giraffe carefully, he followed the delicious view of her red bottom. He adjusted himself roughly before tucking the device into his pocket. This was exquisite torture for him as well.

He crowded into the bathroom after her. "Hold Tiger, Giana. He wanted to give you some love."

She gratefully hugged her long-time buddy to her chest. "Thank you, Daddy."

"You're welcome, Flame." He loved the adorable image.

Grabbing a towel from the rack, Koa spread it lengthwise over the edge of the tub and onto the floor. He spotted her pink razor on a shelf above the tub and relocated it to be handy. Now he was ready for his little girl.

He reached his hand out for hers and drew her to the tub. "Sit on the tub, Flame. Spread your legs wide for Daddy." Koa loved how she followed his directions instantly.

Koa memorized the view. As he took in the sight of her completely exposed, she tentatively drew her knees together. "Wider."

She jumped and moved back into position.

"Good girl. Stay just like that for Daddy."

He dispensed a generous supply of liquid soap from the dispenser onto his hands. Working it between his fingers and adding a bit of water, he created a thick foam. After transferring it to one hand, he rinsed the other and filled a disposable cup halfway with warm water.

"Daddy's going to take off your adult hair. Being bare and sensitive will help you be little," he explained as he lowered himself to one knee before her.

The aroma of her arousal filled his senses. Koa tightened his reserve and steeled himself to finish his mission. He spread the mixture over her skin, coating her entire mound and the edges of her outer lips.

"I could send you to be fully waxed, but I need to keep you to myself. No one needs to see this beautiful sight but me and your doctor, of course," he told her as he picked up the razor and brought it close to her skin. "Don't move, Flame. I don't want to hurt you."

He could feel her body responding to the drag of the razor over her skin. With each stroke, he uncovered more of her tender skin. Koa stroked a fingertip over the shaved strip and loved her shiver as he directly caressed her sensitive skin. Rinsing the razor frequently in the water cup, he smoothed away the silken strands until she sat bare in front of him.

"Stay just like that, little girl."

Koa selected a washcloth from the rack and wet it. He

efficiently cleaned the soap and any remaining pubic hair from her mound, swirling the soft fabric across her sensitive flesh. He threw the cloth into the laundry bin and clamped his hands over her thighs to prevent her move to close her thighs.

"Not yet, Flame."

When her muscles relaxed, he drew the vibrator from his pocket and watched her eyes widen. "I need to check whether this works correctly. If so, we'll take it with us."

"No, Daddy. It's... It's only a toy."

He pressed the button, and the vibration filled the quiet space. "Never tell Daddy no, little girl. You can use your safeword if you need me to stop."

Koa ran the tip over his forearm and down to his fingertip. Her gaze locked on his actions. "Mmm. That feels good, Flame. Let's see if you like it."

He touched the end to her knee and trailed the vibrator down her inner thigh toward her now bare pussy. Focused intently on the device, Giana froze into place as if she'd locked her muscles.

"Breathe, little girl."

She nodded and filled her lungs as the tip drew closer. He traced a path to the top of her cleft and allowed the vibrations to roll through her. That breath gushed from her lips.

"You were a very good girl, taking your spanking and letting Daddy shave you. I think that deserves a reward. Don't you?"

"Please, Daddy. I need to come."

"Let's see if I can help you, Flame."

Koa glided the tip over the edges of her lips before allowing it to slide over her pink folds. Her fingers whitened on Tiger's soft fur as all her muscles tensed. He circled her drenched opening before brushing her vibrator over her clit.

Giana lifted the stuffie to cover her mouth as she

screamed her pleasure into the room. Koa wrapped an arm around her, stabilizing her to prevent her from tumbling off the edge of the tub. She hid her face against his chest as she shook from her orgasm. When he silenced the device, she slumped on his shoulder.

Scooping her up into his arms, Koa carried her back to the bedroom and placed her on the comforter. He folded the material draping over the side of the bed back over her half-nude body. "Rest, Flame. Daddy will take care of everything."

She nodded and rolled onto her side. Curled around her stuffie, the new center of his world closed her eyes. He adjusted her cover, needing to take care of her before forcing himself away.

After dropping her toy onto the packed clothes, Koa moved around the room quietly. Walking into her closet, he selected a few of the work clothes she'd hung as sets. He set those aside. Scanning the rack, he tried to deduce which items she preferred. Koa noticed some articles hung on plain plastic hangers while she'd placed others on special hangers decorated with flowers on the hook. Those must be her favorites.

He filled his arms with an assortment of jeans, tops, and even a jacket. Returning to the bedroom, he heard a faint snore coming from Tiger. Or was that the sweet mouth pressed to him? Delighted by his little girl, Koa hugged her clothing to his chest, allowing himself to celebrate that he'd found her for a few moments.

Finally forcing himself to get to work, he folded the clothes into the suitcase and located a few more things from her dresser. He returned to the bathroom to grab a box of tampons from under the sink. When Koa spotted a travel makeup bag there as well, he placed the assortment of beauty supplies on the vanity inside. With those containers stored for the trip to his place, Koa closed the suitcase and eased the zipper around.

Now to collect Giana. He'd set aside a pair of underwear with cute bunnies scattered on the cotton fabric. Carrying those to her, Koa coaxed her awake. "Time to wake up, Giana. Let's get you dressed."

After a few minutes, he helped her through the door. When she rubbed her eyes, he asked, "Are you awake enough to walk to the truck, little girl? Do you want me to carry you, or should we go back in and let your toy wake you up?"

Giana shook her head and stood straighter. Her eyes opened wide as she shook off the nap. "I can walk. I'm okay."

When she made it to the truck, Koa paused at the passenger door. "Give Daddy a kiss and we'll head home."

She rose on her tiptoes to press her mouth against his. Koa pulled her close and kissed her thoroughly.

"Get a room, slut!"

Koa immediately released Giana and ran toward the blue car. As he touched the driver's door handle, the man stepped on the gas and squealed away. Koa lost his grip but chased the car to the entrance of the apartment complex, successfully memorizing the license plate. After jotting it down on his phone, Koa jogged back to Giana.

"Have you had problems with that jerk before?"

"Well, I've made the jump from bitch to slut," she said offhandedly.

Koa's blood pressure soared at her casual revelation that someone was speaking to his little girl like that. "How long has this been going on?"

"Really, it's nothing. Just a jerk who doesn't like women. He's only said something to me once before. I'd blocked him in the parking lot and pissed him off."

"That act doesn't warrant calling you rude names, Giana," Koa told her.

"I know that, and you know that, but he doesn't. And neither of us is in charge of teaching him. Ignore his bad behavior. I'd say you scared the crap out of him."

"He's lucky I didn't get that door open."

"His eyes got so big," Giana said and chuckled. "I love it when bullies get a dose of their own medicine. Really, Koa, just drop it."

"Daddy."

"Yes, Daddy," she said, rolling her eyes.

"Your cute butt doesn't want another spanking so soon."

"Weren't we going to your house?" she asked.

"Let's get you tucked in the truck and we'll be on our way."

A few minutes later, he shut her door firmly and circled the tailgate to jump into his seat. After leaving the lot, Koa scanned the route and kept an eye on his mirrors for anyone following them. He'd definitely follow up on that guy tomorrow, but for now, getting Giana home was his priority.

CHAPTER 9

By two the next afternoon, Giana had decided she was happier now than she'd ever been before. She'd curled up on Koa's hard chest with his arm wrapped around her as they watched cartoons. Jelly and Tiger were so happy to be together again. They played on the couch next to her, sticking close.

Peeking over at her daddy, she checked to make sure he wasn't getting bored. She suspected Koa hadn't spent too many days vegging out on the couch, but he was an expert at helping her relax and entertaining her with how much he needed to learn about popular programs she loved.

"So, he's a sponge, and he lives under the sea?" Koa double-checked.

"That's right, Daddy. And we're going to see a movie next about a strange dog that lives in Hawaii."

"A blue dog?" Koa asked, obviously trying hard to remember all she'd taught him that morning.

"Yes. But not the blue dog that lives in Australia. That's a different show," she reminded him.

"Right," he said, drawing out that word as if he was totally confused. "You'd better hang around for a while, so I get all of this straight."

"Okay, Daddy. I can do that." She stretched up to kiss the corner of his mouth, but Koa turned his head to meet her lips fully. "Mmm," she hummed as the heat built between them.

She jerked away when his phone blared the national anthem. "Who's that?"

"Jerico or Caden. Let's see who's inviting us to dinner."

Koa answered the phone. "Hi, Caden. Barbecue at your house tonight? I'm supposed to pick up a dessert the girls would enjoy." He looked at Giana to check whether she'd want to go. "Pippa and Aspen are going to be there?"

Giana nodded quickly. She'd love to see her friends and spend some time with their daddies as well as the other men on the team.

"Count us in. Are you sure you don't want me to bring wings?" he joked.

Giana shook her head vigorously and then chuckled as she realized that had become a joke with the others. Her daddy was amazing and didn't have any trouble making fun of himself or admitting he'd screwed up.

When he disconnected from the call, Koa asked, "What kind of dessert should we pick up?"

"Cookies and ice cream. We had a big debate over what flavor of each treat combines to make the best cookiewiches."

"Sounds like the three of you enjoy each other's company."

"We do. We have a lot in common and enough differences that we don't bore each other. Both Pippa and Aspen think you're great. Not as handsome as their daddies, but what do they know?"

"Yeah, what do they know?" Koa repeated, grinning at her.

He had no idea how hot he was when he smiled like that.

It did all sorts of things to her tummy inside each time. Squeezing her thighs together, she felt the simmering arousal that had lingered from simply being close to him flare higher. She whirled her fingertip in the silky strands on his chest.

"Maybe we should take a nap if we're going to a party tonight?" she suggested.

"That's a good idea," he agreed immediately and scooped her onto his lap. Standing, he carried her back to his room and pulled her T-shirt over her head. Koa cupped her bare breasts, running his rough thumbs over her nipples.

Instantly, that growing heat combusted to need. She swayed closer, pressing her breasts fully into his hands. Koa's fingers trailed down to her waistband and unfastened her shorts.

"I have to be naked to nap?" Giana asked, playfully batting her eyes at him.

"It's the nap law. You can ask your friends tonight if you need to check."

"I can't ask them that!"

"Of course you can. You could ask their daddies if you prefer…" Koa's voice faded away as he drew her shorts and panties to her ankles.

"I'll ask Pippa and Aspen," she rushed to assure him.

"Good idea." He tapped her foot, signaling for her to lift it.

"Has everyone had a little girl before?" Giana asked, stepping out of her clothing.

"Yes. In various degrees of seriousness. Somehow everyone on the team is a committed daddy. I don't know if our similar preferences make us work better together automatically, or if our daddy sides bond us closer so we synchronize on a higher level. Either way, I've never seen a group operate as well as we do."

"I'm glad, Daddy. I want you to come home safely." Giana's eyes filled with tears. She'd avoided thinking of the possibility of Koa not returning from a mission. As a person with a high-risk job herself, Giana thought she was immune from worrying about what could happen tomorrow. That invulnerability flew out the window when she thought about Koa.

"Hey, Flame. It's okay, baby." He stood and scooped her up in his arms. He sat on the side of the bed to cradle her, rocking her slowly. "Shh!"

"I-I'm sorry," Giana choked out.

"Thank you for caring about me, Flame. I worry about you too. I'd wish we both had boring desk jobs, but I don't think we'd be happy there."

"No. That would be torture," she admitted, wiping the tears from her cheeks.

"No one knows when it's their time to go. We need to treasure every day we have together, little girl."

He kissed her softly as he stroked her hair. "You are so precious to me. Is it too quick for me to tell you I love you, Giana?"

The breath caught in her chest as she studied his face. She couldn't detect any sign of fakery or deceit. His expression was caring and open. "You love me?" she asked.

"With all my heart, Giana."

She struggled with what to say. Huge feelings toward him filled her, but she wasn't ready to tell him yet. "I…"

He kissed her, stopping her from talking. His lips moved softly on hers. Wooing and tempting her to focus only on the kiss. His hands moved on her skin, stroking and caressing her as if he had a million minutes and wanted to spend all of them with her.

Giana wrapped her arms around his neck and abandoned

herself to the sensations he created. Pushing away her awkwardness and previous sadness, Koa forced her to focus on the now—to enjoy the sweet heat that he built inside her.

Koa leaned back, carrying her with him as he reclined on the bed. Giana squirmed on top of him, turning to stretch herself over him. She pressed her knees into the mattress, straddling his pelvis. A low moan burst from her lips as his thick cock slid against her intimately.

"You have too many clothes on," she protested and scooted off Koa to tug at his shorts.

Helping her, Koa lifted his hips, allowing her to draw the cotton fabric over his impressive shaft. She'd never get used to seeing his body. Chiseled and toned, Koa was pure power filling in a handsome wrapper. His island ancestry gave him an exotic flair that set him apart from others.

She tossed away the material in her hands as Koa got rid of the T-shirt he'd removed for her. "You are so hot," she whispered, running her hands over his muscles. She pressed a kiss to his chest and daringly whisked her tongue over his nipple.

His low moan pushed her arousal even higher. Nothing was off limits with Koa. He made her want to try everything.

She trailed her fingers down the center of his chest and hesitated just shy of his erection. "Um, can I kiss you here, Daddy?"

His cock jerked as she watched, and Giana flicked her short nails along his skin, getting dangerously close to touching him.

"I would love to feel your lips on my cock, Flame. Turn around and straddle my face."

"What?" She looked at him in shock. He didn't mean what she thought he did… Did he?

"Come here, Giana. I need a taste of your honey as you explore."

Koa gripped her hips and moved Giana effortlessly to face down the length of his body. Then he helped her scoot over his face into the position he desired with her calves tucked under his arms. Sexual heat had to radiate down to him as she hovered over him. Giana started to close her eyes, imagining the view he must have, but noticed her own.

She lowered herself, licking the length of his shaft from base to tip. When he cursed behind her, she knew he enjoyed her caresses. Giana swirled her tongue around the velvety head and felt his fingers tighten on her hips. The slight touch of pain added to the sensual experience. She'd remember this moment each time she spotted a bruise.

"I'm not going to last long like this, Flame. Stop when I tell you. I want to come buried deep inside your heat."

Giana wrapped her lips around his shaft and hummed her agreement. "Um-hmmm."

His grip tightened, and he drew her pussy to his lips. He nibbled and tasted her, making her eyes cross with the sensations. Struggling to remember her goal to drive him crazy as he pushed every blooming thought from her mind, Giana gripped the base of his shaft firmly and slid her mouth over his cock. Swallowing his entire erection would be impossible, but she was going to try her best.

Sensual sounds filled the surrounding space, adding to the eroticism of their lovemaking. Giana abandoned all embarrassment and inhibitions and focused only on the pleasure they created. Vivid tingles heralded her approaching climax, and Giana focused on driving him crazy.

His roar made Giana lift her head away from his shaft. That was the only warning she got. Koa tossed her safely onto her back on the mattress and pounced. Moving with tiger-like grace, he thrust fully into her, stretching and filling Giana. Instantly, her approaching orgasm exploded, and her body tightened around him.

"Giana!" he shouted as his hot cum filled her. His thrusts never paused until her pleasure ignited into a second body-shaking sensation.

"Daddy!" she whispered, clinging tightly to him.

When his heart rate slowed, Koa shifted their bodies under the covers. Giana curled against him, closing her eyes. She didn't understand how being with him could be so magical, but she hoped this would never end.

* * *

Holding her sexy daddy's hand made walking through the grocery store a lot more fun. She'd offered to make a dessert, but Koa had vetoed that idea. They'd already picked out three types of cookies and were on their way to pick out some ice cream flavors.

"Hi!" a cute brunette wearing a bikini top and low-slung micro jean shorts greeted Koa. Giana noticed the woman studiously avoided meeting her gaze but focused on the soldier next to her.

"Ma'am," Koa politely acknowledged her as he continued down the aisle.

"I don't suppose you'd grab that box on the top shelf for me?" the woman asked, pointing into the freezer at something literally at her eye level.

"Oh, you must be allergic to cold. Let me get that for you. Go ahead, Koa. I'll meet you there," Giana said, opening the clear door. She noticed Koa walked a few feet, but turned to focus on the shelves, keeping Giana in his view.

"Oh. I didn't mean for you to get it for me," the woman said with a sour expression.

"You're welcome. I enjoy doing things for others who have problems," Giana said cheerfully as she handed over the box of frozen dog treats.

"I don't have a problem," the shopper retorted.

"Oh, good. I hope your dog loves those," Giana said and walked away with a fake friendly wave.

"Dog treats?" the woman mumbled. "They make that crap?"

Giana heard the door reopen, and the woman slammed the box back on the shelf. Slapping a hand over her mouth to control her giggles, Giana rejoined Koa. He smacked her bottom smartly while the woman was distracted.

"Hey!"

"You are being bad, little girl."

"She deserved every bit of that." Giana projected her voice louder and back toward the flirtatious female. "I didn't tell her about the huge smudge of mascara under her eye."

Out of the corner of her vision, Giana saw the woman pull her sunglasses down from their perch on her head to shield her eyes. Giana couldn't help smirking when she stomped away.

"Hey!" Giana protested when her daddy swatted her one more time. "She deserved all of that."

"She might have, but you don't need to worry about anyone else," Koa assured her. "I've found my little girl and I won't risk losing you."

"Sorry, Daddy. I should have ignored her."

"Let's go choose some ice cream for the party. They're going to wonder where we are."

"Cookies and cream is my favorite. Pippa likes vanilla and chocolate, so she'll love that flavor. Can we get chocolate with chocolate chips for Aspen? She's like an over-the-top chocolate fanatic."

"Sounds like a great plan. I like cookies and cream, too."

"Of course you do, Daddy. We're soulmates."

Koa nodded and hugged her close to his side. "We are, Flame. And very lucky."

Giana pressed a kiss to his shoulder as they stopped to grab the ice cream. She wished time would freeze. She'd never been this happy before. Crossing her fingers at her side, Giana hoped with everything inside her that nothing would ruin this. She'd never survive losing Koa.

"Whatever that thought was, get rid of it," Koa ordered firmly.

When she glanced up at him in surprise, he squeezed her close again. "Let's go join our friends."

"I'd like that."

In a few minutes, Koa pulled into an already packed driveway. Giana reached for the door handle, eager to go see her friends. Koa's powerful hand clamped over her thigh, stopping her.

"Daddy will open your door, little girl."

"But I have hands. I've opened my door a billion times."

"Not when you're with your daddy. You will wait for me to help you out."

She stared at him in exasperation. "Fine."

"Improve that attitude or I'll borrow Caden's guest room to wipe your grumpiness away," Koa warned.

"What? How would you do that?"

"By turning my sullen little girl over my knee and turning her bottom right red."

Giana stared at him, snapping her jaw closed when she realized it gaped open. "You'd spank me here?"

"Yes."

His tone didn't contain a maybe. She looked down the driveway at Caden's house. Koa had shared they were all daddies. The other two women had shared that they were little. Did that mean that at any of their houses, Koa's dominance would be in full force?

She refocused on Koa. "You're my daddy with them?"

"I'm your daddy at all times, but yes, we can be ourselves here without judgment."

"Can I come sit on your lap?"

"I would love that, Flame."

"Koa, I trust you. If anything got out about me being little at the fire station, I'd lose my position. No one would follow my directions."

"My team would jump on a grenade to save you, Giana. They're never going to out you. But you get to decide to act as you wish. Why not see what feels right?"

"You'll support me either way?"

"Without question. You're my little girl whether you are in little mode or a kickass fire captain. I love you, Giana."

"I can't believe I feel this strongly after such a short time."

Koa pushed his seat back and plucked her out of her spot. Settling her on his lap, he kissed her until they both breathed heavily. "Maybe we should go back home."

A knock on the window made Giana jump. They turned to see Pippa standing beside the truck.

Koa laughed and opened the door.

"You're letting the ice cream melt," Pippa teased.

"Oh! The ice cream! We have to get it inside." Giana panicked and scooted toward the opening. Her hand landed dangerously close to her daddy's privates.

"Whoa! Let me help you."

Koa wrapped an arm around Giana's waist and swung her down to stand next to a giggling Pippa who seemed to know exactly what had happened. Pippa hugged her tightly and stepped back to take her hand.

"Come on, Giana. Aspen is in timeout. I've been so bored for three whole minutes. Come play with me!" Pippa pleaded.

"I'll bring in the ice cream. You go with Pippa."

"Thanks…" Giana hesitated for a minute before adding, "Daddy."

"Come on, Giana. I brought my stuffie to show you."

Giana looked over her shoulder as she allowed Pippa to tug her toward the house. Koa mouthed, "Good girl," to her. He recognized how brave she had chosen to be.

CHAPTER 10

Giana, Pippa, Aspen, and the latter's faithful dog, Rexy, sat in the blanket fort Jerico had created for them over four lawn chairs. He'd even equipped it with a small rotating fan to circulate a breeze in the summer evening heat. The three women sat eating their concocted ice cream cookiewiches.

Rexy as usual didn't beg for food. Aspen had explained earlier about the abuse the sweet canine had suffered from his first owner. He simply lay on the blanket close to his rescuer getting frequent pets from all three little girls.

"I love Rexy," Giana said and took another bite of her treat.

"He's a sweetheart. I love this dessert, Giana," Aspen congratulated her.

"It is yummy!" Pippa agreed.

"Mmm." Giana nodded in agreement with her mouth full.

"How are things with your daddy?" Pippa asked.

Giana held up a finger to ask for a second and finished chewing her bite. It gave her a few seconds to think as well. She swallowed and smiled. "I'm so happy."

The others beamed back at her. "That's awesome," Aspen said.

"I didn't know what having a daddy full-time would be like. I mean it's only been a few days, but I love how much he cares about me."

"We've enjoyed this break as well," Aspen shared, waggling her eyebrows suggestively.

The woman giggled at her funny expressions.

"They won't be sent away soon, will they? I wanted to ask when I saw Koa repacking his supplies." Their expressions answered Giana without either woman saying a word. "I was afraid of that."

"That's the tough part of having a daddy who's a soldier," Aspen admitted.

"And the best part?" Giana asked.

"The best eye candy ever," Pippa answered without hesitation.

"Definitely," Aspen agreed, doing that thing with her eyebrows again.

This time, their laughter was a bit louder, attracting attention from the men sitting a short distance away.

"They're talking about us, aren't they?" Giana recognized Koa's voice and heard the amusement in it.

"Oh, yeah. Talking about their daddies is a favorite topic," Zale said.

"Only because you're so cute, Daddy!" Pippa called out to him.

"Thank you, Kitten. Are you drinking your water?" Zale asked.

Pippa picked up her water bottle he'd reminded her to take into the fort and displayed it for the others. It had maybe a few sips missing. "Yes, Daddy. I'm working on it." She unscrewed the top and took a big drink.

"That's my good girl," he answered.

"He's always on me to drink water. Yuck. It's so boring," Pippa said quietly so the men wouldn't overhear.

"I've drunk more milk since meeting Koa than I have in twenty years," Giana confessed. "I'm concerned. I'm starting to like it."

"Definitely my daddy makes healthier choices for me than I do for myself," Aspen admitted.

"Do you feel better?" Giana asked.

"I do," Pippa piped in. "Of course, my daddy is the medic. He takes care of everything to do with my body. Even when I don't want him to."

Aspen nodded sympathetically. "I bet. I always feel better when Daddy calls Zale to come over and check me out. But… after the treatment."

"Wait. Why does Zale come over to check you out?" Giana asked.

"He is the team medic. He's a nurse practitioner—the highest level of nurse. Kind of like a doctor-light. He can prescribe medicine and have tests run. He keeps the guys healthy on missions and when they're home, too. My daddy trusts Zale so much—and he's great. He helped with birth control, random things like an ear infection, and when my tummy gets wonky," Aspen shared.

"He, like, examines you? Or just prescribes some generic type of medicine?" Giana asked.

"Examines, pokes, prods, and treats," Aspen admitted.

Giana turned to Pippa. "Isn't that weird?" Her thoughts jumbled inside her brain as she tried to understand and not panic.

"You mean Zale seeing Aspen naked? It bothered me in the beginning, but I realized he sees the guys naked, too. He's seen a lot of people without clothes on, and he chose me."

That made some sense to Giana; even so, she wasn't sure she'd be that okay with it.

"Besides, I like Aspen. I don't want her ear to hurt or for her to be worried about getting pregnant if she's not ready for that," Pippa told her.

"Zale's great. He's better than any doctor I've ever had, and my daddy can stay with me, and no one thinks it's weird," Aspen added.

"Is my daddy going to want me to see Zale, too?" Giana asked. She tried to keep the nervousness out of her voice. Giana definitely hadn't considered that someone she saw frequently would get to see all of her.

"Probably, but you should talk to him about it if you're concerned," Pippa told her. "Daddies are perceptive, but sometimes they don't know you're worried unless you tell them. Littles are good at hiding their feelings from others."

"Probably because we're so used to hiding who we are from the world," Aspen guessed.

"I'm glad I get to be myself around you both. If it's okay, I need to be close to my daddy now," Giana confessed.

"Go, Giana. We'll come with you. I could use a cuddle myself," Pippa admitted.

"Me too."

In a flash, they crawled out from under the blanket. Each walked quickly to their daddy's chair.

Trailing the others, Giana watched out of the corner of her eye and saw Zale and Jerico scoop up their Littles to sit on their laps. Neither asked any questions, but simply welcomed their little girl happily.

"Daddy?" she whispered.

"Come here, Flame. I missed you." Koa lifted her onto his hard thighs and squeezed her gently. He pressed a kiss to that sensitive spot under her ear and asked, "You okay?"

She nodded and tucked her head into the hollow in the curve of his shoulder. The reassuringly regular thump of her daddy's heartbeat sounded under her ear. Koa rubbed her back, not asking questions, but letting her process through her thoughts and feelings. She pressed a kiss to his skin.

"Need to go home, Giana?" he asked softly.

"No, Daddy. I just needed you."

Koa answered that confession with a kiss on her forehead and a pat on her bottom. Conversation hummed over and around her. Giana could feel the camaraderie and how much these men cared about each other. Teasing remarks were free of animosity, and the response from each man felt real. There was nothing fake here.

A feeling of calm serenity filled her. Giana hadn't ever been this comfortable amid others. Sleeping at the fire station was always a challenge for her. She usually doubled up on caffeine and took power naps. Nothing had ever happened to her. Having people around at her most vulnerable kept her from being able to relax. The deep men's voices blended together into an attractive hum.

* * *

"Daddy's getting up, Flame. It's time for little girls to be in bed," Koa whispered to her as he tightened his arms around her.

As he stood, Giana wrapped her arms around Koa's neck to stabilize herself. Blinking into the dim light provided by the fire pit, Giana struggled to figure out what was going on. "Daddy?"

"Hi, sweetheart. Hold on to Daddy. We're heading home," Koa told her gently.

"I'll get the chair for you, Koa. Carry your Little to the truck," a familiar voice said softly.

"Thanks, Hank. I owe you one," Koa answered as he walked toward the corner of the house.

"I can walk," Giana told him.

"I know, Flame. Maybe Daddy wants to carry you."

"Okay, Daddy." She laid her head back on his shoulder. "So sleepy."

"Daddy kept you out too late."

"Mmmhmm."

He jostled her a bit as he opened the truck door. The interior light glared in her eyes as he set her bottom in the seat. Giana covered her eyes with her hands to block it out. Koa gently tugged her hands away to buckle her seatbelt when he had her facing the front.

When his heat moved away, she missed him immediately. The solid thunk of the door closing sounded next, and the light dwindled out. She peeked from under her hand only to slap her fingers back over her eyes as it flared back to life when he opened the driver's side.

"Rude," she grumbled.

"Sorry, little girl. I'll put an eye mask in here next time. Close your eyes and drift back to sleep."

"Okay, Daddy."

It seemed only a few seconds later that darn light was back in her eyes. "Daddy!" she whined, burying her face against the seat's upholstery.

"Come on, Flame. Let's get you into bed."

He picked her up. Giana wrapped her legs around his waist and looped her arms around his neck, trusting him completely. In a short time, he had showered away the remnants of being outdoors and brushed her teeth.

"Go to sleep, little girl. I'll go check all the doors and I'll be back."

Turning onto her tummy, Giana drifted into dreams of sweet desserts and good friends.

CHAPTER 11

The loud ringing of Giana's phone woke them at three a.m. Instantly, his little girl rolled out of bed and ran for the device plugged into the nearby charging station.

"This is Captain Mancini."

Koa turned on the bedside lamp and watched his little girl's usually expressive face. It was deadpan serious as she listened to whoever had called.

"Contact stations ten and thirteen. Ask them to respond to the scene with safety equipment for unfriendlies. Do not resume battling the fire until the police have the scene under control. I will be there in eight minutes."

She disconnected from the call and raced into the closet. Koa slid out of bed and pulled on a pair of shorts. Giana emerged fully dressed, carrying her boots. "Can I borrow socks? I forgot those."

"Of course." Koa opened a drawer and found a pair of tube socks. Tossing them to her as she sat on the bed, he asked, "Can you tell me what's happening?"

"There's a big warehouse fire. Seems deliberately set with

an accelerant. Two of my guys are down after being grazed with bullets. Thankfully, nothing serious."

"Someone is shooting at them while the team is trying to put the fire out?" Koa asked in disbelief.

"A sniper. They can't figure out exactly where he is, but the police are on the scene. I'm headed to liaison with them and support the firefighters."

"Hank is our sniper. He's an expert in pinpointing the location. I'll have him meet you there."

Giana hesitated for a minute, and Koa guessed she was battling how to separate work life from home. "If he's available and willing, have him ask for me at the barricade. It's a dangerous situation."

"Got it. Be safe, Flame. I just found you."

"I'll update you when I can."

Koa walked her to the door and watched her back out into the darkness. He was used to seeing danger from the other side. It gave him a better perspective of how military spouses worried at deployment.

Forcing himself into action, Koa ran back to grab his phone.

"Koa! What's up? Did I miss a deployment call?" Hank sounded completely alert.

"No, Hank. It's something personal. Giana received a call from the station. The firefighters are under attack from a sniper. The police are on the scene, but they can't locate the source."

"Text me the address. I'll grab my scope and go help. Giana's okay?"

"She's fine. Two grazed by bullets. No serious injuries."

"Either someone seriously skilled and trying to torment them or a novice who got ahold of a weapon. Either is dangerous."

"I know." Koa's last attempt to prevent himself from worrying evaporated at Hank's blunt assessment.

"Text me the address. I'll update you when I can."

* * *

Koa paced the length of his open living room and kitchen area. He had to stop himself repeatedly from grabbing his keys and racing his truck down to the scene. Okay, he'd already stuffed his keyring in his pocket, but he was still inside.

His phone buzzed with an incoming message. He looked at the screen to see a message from Hank.

Sniper located and in custody.

Thank goodness. Wait, was Giana okay? He was typing an answer back to his teammate, when another message appeared.

Turn on the morning news.

He snatched the remote from the coffee table and navigated through the screens to find the local news station. Giana's beautiful face filled his screen. Relief flooded through him as Koa sank down on the couch to listen.

"...firefighters are now able to battle the blaze without risk of being killed. The delay in dealing with the fire allowed the flames to jump to two other buildings. I have called in three other stations to assist us. This will be a total loss for all three structures, but if we're lucky, we'll contain it there."

"Have the authorities identified the shooter or determined his motives?" a news reporter asked, shoving her mic into Giana's face.

Giana put her hand over the device and pushed it away from her lips. Even from the video, Koa noted Giana's lethal glare she used to target the offensive woman. "I will provide you with details as I address all the media sources. Do not jab this into my face."

Focusing back on the group, she continued, "I do not have definitive information on the shooter at this point. The police will take the podium next. I would like to thank a Special Ops officer from the local base for assisting the officers and protecting the firefighters. His skill facilitated locating the culprit. Everyone will make it home to their families because of him."

"What's his name?" the same reporter asked again, rudely pushing her microphone too close to Giana.

His beloved fire captain plucked the device from the reporter's hand and tossed it over her head to a fireman standing behind her. Koa recognized him. It was the one who'd glared daggers at him when Koa had appeared at the station. The man caught it easily and stuck it inside his protective gear.

Koa grinned at the screen. *Take that, obnoxious reporter.* He enjoyed seeing Giana in her official role and understood why she'd achieved her rank in the fire department at a younger age than most captains. She didn't put up with any crap. It pleased him to see her firefighters supporting her without question.

"I understand you have a job to do, but I'm only going to warn you once before I eliminate the problem," Giana said firmly. She continued with her briefing without skipping a beat.

He liked that his little girl was a badass at work. Koa watched the last of the program hoping to see Giana for an update. Now the live segments focused on the firefighters battling the blaze. He caught a glimpse of Giana coordinating from the sidelines several times.

A few minutes later, the footage brought him to his feet as he saw Giana scaling a ladder over a flare of fire. Koa paced along the width of the house, following the next segment to make sure she was fine. When the morning news coverage ended, he checked online to see if there was an update. Nothing.

The ringing of his doorbell made him jump. Koa shook his head as he walked to answer it. His nerves were usually rock steady.

"Hank?" Koa stared at his teammate. "What's going on? Is something wrong with Giana?"

"She was fine when I left her. They're going to be on scene for a long time, putting out that fire. We knew you'd be tense," Hank said and waved a hand toward the rest of the team, who stood in his driveway. "Come on. We're going on a run."

"I thought we had the day off," Koa said, staring at the group.

"We do. This is to save your sanity and for fun for the rest of us. You've got three minutes before we start, then you have to race to catch up to us."

When Koa hesitated, Caden called, "Time starts now."

Koa didn't wait to see him click the timer on his watch. He raced toward the bedroom, yanking off his slouchy clothes to grab training gear like the others wore. He knelt on the doorstep, tying his shoelaces as Caden took off with the others falling into step behind him.

"Fuck!" Koa secured his other shoe and sped off to join his team. At about mile three, his body released the tension that had built from worrying about Giana. That didn't mean he forgot to check his phone for messages.

Jerico turned into a parking lot, and the other guys cheered. Koa glanced up to read the name of a climbing gym he'd always wanted to check out. "We're going in here?" Koa asked.

"Caden arranged for us to challenge ourselves in return for some shooting instruction for the owner and a few friends," Hank explained. "It seemed like a good time to come."

"This absolutely rocks," Koa said, eagerly following the others to the door. Just as he walked in, his phone buzzed. He looked down at the screen to see his little girl's photo.

"Giana," he called and walked back outside. "Hey, Flame. Are you okay?"

"Sooty and buried in paperwork. I'll be here for several hours talking to the higher-ups and filling in forms," she reported.

"I can handle having my own s'more," he teased, feeling the last of his worry subside. Koa kept his voice light, not wanting her to know how much the danger in her job affected him. "Did you ever give that microphone back?"

"That reporter always does that. This was the fourth microphone I've taken from her."

Koa could hear the aggravation in her voice and guessed that a massive eye roll had accompanied it. "I'm glad you're okay, Flame."

"Hank was invaluable. Thank him for me." She paused as a big group emerged from the climbing gym, talking animatedly. "Where are you?"

"The team guessed I needed to let some steam off. We ran to the new rock-climbing place. I'm standing outside."

"Go! You can't let them get ahead of you," Giana said.

He laughed. She knew him too well. The competition among the team members was fierce in training. They all pushed each other to the highest level. "You won't be home for a while?"

"I've got at least two hours here. Probably three because I'm fielding phone calls as well."

"I'll meet you at home."

"Sounds good. Go have fun," she urged and hung up before he could say anything else.

Jogging inside, he found the team already scaling the wall in two teams. "A race?" he asked.

"You're with us, Koa," Jerico told him, pointing to the empty protective gear waiting for him.

In a flash, Koa donned the harness and strapped his helmet on. He studied the wall and watched Zale already in progress. When he reached too far for his next handhold, Koa yelled, "Go for the red peg, Zale."

The team's medic immediately took his advice and shifted to that one. He reached the top a few seconds before Jerico. "Gotcha!" Zale celebrated and scrambled back down to the floor.

As he stepped out of the way, Jerico attacked the wall. Koa scrutinized his style, noting his climbing strength. About halfway, Koa called to Jerico, "Grab the yellow to your right and then step on the blue."

It would require great hip flexibility for Jerico to stretch a leg up that far, but if he was successful, Jerico could power upward, skipping two steps. Jerico reached for the yellow and missed it. Holding his breath, Koa watched Jerico adjust slightly before shifting his weight. It took a couple of seconds more for the tricky maneuver, but Jerico powered up into the lead and tapped the ceiling.

As soon as Jerico stepped away from the wall, Koa scampered up, making it look effortless. He tapped the ceiling when Max had reached the halfway mark. Koa passed him on the way down and patted his back as the large man powered upward.

"What are you? Part mountain goat?" Max demanded.

"I think we've found our rock-climbing expert. That's an excellent skill for the team," Caden commented as Koa's team high-fived each other.

"I grew up climbing rock faces in Hawaii," Koa said.

"Can you give the rest of us some pointers?" Caden asked. "I'd love to see all of us increase our speed."

"Of course. The key is capitalizing on our natural talents. For example, Jerico is nimble. He does best when he makes big moves upward—lifting his foot to a step at his collarbone level. That boosts him tremendously instead of taking smaller steps," Koa explained.

"What's your advice for me?" Max asked.

"You have massive strength in your shoulders. Reach as high as you can and power upward," Koa suggested. "Try it."

Max immediately returned to the wall and jumped to reach a grip with his left hand. He steadied himself with his right hand and then pushed off footholds to propel himself upward. Koa helped him choose suitable targets as Max tried the new system. He reached the top in a much shorter time.

"That's impressive, Koa," the big man said when he once again stood with the group. "I would have said I always use my arm strength, but you shifted my grip, forcing me to use my shoulders and back. That was more efficient."

"Well, do me next," Caden requested. "What do you suggest?"

One by one, Koa worked with everyone. Each member of the team reduced their time and gained new insight. They'd all done climbing with ropes or scaling flat walls. This was a new format for them to adjust to. Koa helped each make the most of their skills while dangling from finger holds.

By the time Caden called an end to their fun, Koa's muscles quivered from the intense workout. As everyone moved arms and legs to stretch, Koa was sure he wouldn't be the only one who would feel the effects of this afternoon. They were getting ready to run back to Koa's when his phone rang.

"Giana? Are you headed home?"

"I'm actually in the parking lot. When I saw everyone's car at your house, I thought you might want a ride," Giana said.

"Giana's here with her truck. Anybody want a ride?" Koa asked the group.

Everyone looked at Caden. The man in charge of their training was notorious for pushing them hard.

"It's supposed to be our day off. I think we can hitch a ride," Caden announced.

Everyone patted Caden on the back as they tromped out to the truck. Piling into the cab and the truck bed, the team filled the space. Koa made sure to be next to his little girl in the cab.

CHAPTER 12

*A*fter parking her truck, Giana took a moment to gather her energy. She hoped Koa would understand that she was completely wiped out. All she wanted to do was wash the smoke smell out of her hair and crawl into bed. The quiet thunk of his door closing made her look toward the now-empty passenger seat.

She checked the mirror and saw him circle the back of the truck and arrive at her door. When he opened it, she rushed to say, "Koa, I'm…"

"Daddy," he corrected gently and reached in to unfasten her seatbelt before scooping her up in his arms. "Come on, little girl. Let's get cleaned up and take a nap."

She wanted to suggest something else he might rather do, but that sounded heavenly. After nodding, she rested her cheek on his shoulder as he carried her into the house. "Daddy," she whispered.

"Have you eaten?"

"No. That fire burned so hot. We roasted in our gear. I couldn't imagine eating." Some of the guys had iron stomachs, and they'd refueled while she was filling out forms.

They'd brought her a sandwich, but the thought of taking a bite made her stomach roll.

"We'll get some nutrition in you before you sleep," Koa promised.

She nodded. "Shower, Daddy."

"Bath, Flame," he suggested as they walked down the hall to the large bathroom.

"Not hot," she pleaded.

"Cool. It will help bring your temperature down. Trust your daddy."

"Will you wash my hair? It smells like smoke."

"Of course. Daddy's going to get every part of you clean."

That promise made her stomach do another flip-flop. Not the bad kind that made her sick, but the type that kindled a different type of fire inside her. She couldn't believe she could even consider hanky-panky. But her body was all in—especially when Koa sat her on the side of the tub and turned to start the water.

She reached out to pat his hard butt. It felt amazing. Her face heated as he stood back up to look at her.

"I'm glad you're recovering. Let's get you in the tub and find some toys for you to play with instead of Daddy's butt."

"No toys are finer than that," she assured him and her face flamed even hotter.

"Thank you, little girl. I like your bottom as well. Now, let's get you undressed and in the tub."

Koa undressed her carefully, running his fingers over her skin to check for any injuries or hot spots. That sensation in her tummy grew hotter as he examined her. When her clothes lay scattered on the floor, Koa lifted her into the tub and helped her settle before turning off the water. The liquid flowed around her, feeling delicious as it cooled her fever.

Giana settled back against the tub, loving the additional chill of the porcelain. Koa knelt by her side, gently sloshing cool water over her skin. A deep sigh eased from her lips as she relaxed. The pressure and worry of the day floated away on the surface of the water as it lapped over her.

"This is heaven," she whispered.

"Good. Scoot down and wet your hair, Flame. Let's wash away the smokiness first."

She nodded and slid her bottom along the tub to dunk her head under the water. When she emerged, Koa handed her a soft, dry washcloth.

"Hold this over your eyes, little girl."

When Giana had followed his instructions, Koa poured a bit of shampoo from the bottle she'd brought from home and rubbed it over her tresses and scalp with firm but gentle fingertips. She loved the feel of having her hair washed. "You are so good at that."

"I have three younger sisters. They trained me well."

"Really? Are you the only boy in your family?" Giana asked, peeking from under the washcloth.

"Keep that in place, little girl. You don't want soap in your eyes," he told her firmly.

Immediately, Giana followed his instruction. "So? Are you the only son?"

"I am. I'm twenty-seven. My sisters are twenty-five, twenty-three, and twenty-one."

"I'm older than you?" she asked, shocked.

"Age doesn't matter to me, Flame. Is it important to you?" he asked.

She noticed he didn't ask how old she was. "Well, it kind of matters. Twenty years from now when I'm talking about the music I listened to in high school, you won't recognize any of the artists."

"I like that thought. I'm glad you're planning to stay with me for twenty years," he commented, totally missing her point.

"No, I mean we won't have anything in common."

"We'll have twenty years in common," he pointed out before adding, "besides, these were probably your favorite groups in high school." Koa named off four bands she'd loved.

"That's impressive. How did you know?"

"Lean back. Let's rinse the suds away. Do you like conditioner?"

"No, thank you. I have a leave-in one that I like," Giana answered before following his directions. His fingers swishing her hair through the water felt magical. Giana could feel her tight shoulder muscles relaxing.

After the stressful day, she'd tensed up even more when she'd realized she was five years older than Koa. He oozed confidence and control—probably a result of his training and skills. Perhaps he was right—the difference in their age didn't matter.

"Up you go, little girl," he said, lifting her easily to sit in the tub. Koa steadied her before wrapping her wet hair in a towel, turban-style, like he'd done that a million times.

"You're thinking too hard, little girl. Are you okay?" Koa asked, pulling the washcloth away from her eyes.

"Sorry. I didn't mean to get lost in my head."

"Being quiet is fine, Flame. Unless you're worrying about something that isn't important."

"Like our age?" she asked.

"Exactly. Our private business is ours."

Koa dipped the washcloth into the water, saturating it. He added some floral-scented soap and stroked the cloth over her back. The sensation of the pull of the terrycloth over her skin mesmerized her. She leaned into his touch.

"That's it, little girl. Just let me take over."

After the day she'd had, releasing control to him was surprisingly easy. Giana realized she trusted Koa. She could allow her inner self to come out safely around him. He kissed her forehead, making her heart melt.

"I've got you, Giana."

"Thank you, Daddy."

By the time he'd washed every inch of her body, Giana was half asleep. Koa dried her skin and wrapped her in a towel. She lolled against his hard muscles as he carried her to the bedroom and tucked her under the covers.

"Don't leave," she whispered as he eased off the bed.

"I'll be right back, Flame."

"Promise?"

"Yes, little girl."

She hovered on the brink of sleep, fighting to stay awake when he returned. "Daddy," she whispered. "I thought you'd forgotten me."

"Never, Giana." He settled on the pillows next to her and wrapped an arm around Giana to slide her closer to him. "I want you to try this, little girl. You need some nourishment. Then you can sleep."

He brushed something rubbery over her lips. "Open your mouth, Flame." When she followed his directions, he inserted the nipple.

She pushed at the alien thing in her mouth. A small drizzle of delicious liquid landed on her tongue. "Mmm," she hummed and tried it again. Wanting more, she sucked tentatively, and her mouth filled with the tasty concoction. Giana swallowed quickly and devoured more.

"That's it, Flame. Drink your bottle for Daddy."

By the time the bottle was empty, Giana's struggle to keep her eyes open had evaporated. Koa removed the nipple from her mouth and replaced it with something that filled her mouth as well, but didn't hold any of the scrumptious formula.

"More, Daddy," she mumbled around the device.

"Not right now, Giana. Your tummy is full." He stroked a hand down her silky skin to rub her stomach softly.

"I'll make you a bottle when you wake up," he promised and rocked her slowly against him. "Sleep, Flame."

* * *

WHEN SHE WOKE UP, Giana couldn't move. Jelly and Tiger had crowded onto the bed and weighed her down. She struggled out of the tightly tucked sheet. When she'd freed her arms, Giana picked up each stuffie and kissed its fuzzy head before setting them aside. Koa had bracketed her with large pillows smooshed tightly at her sides. She attempted to push the fluffy obstacles away, but Koa must have used Daddy magic to pin her in place. Giving up, she called, "Daddy! I'm stuck!"

Almost instantly, she heard the whisper of his light steps in the hallway. "Hi, Flame. I'm glad you're awake."

When Koa whisked away the fluffy pillows holding her in place, she asked, "Why did you do that?"

"I didn't want you to fall out of bed, little girl. I've ordered a crib for you."

"A crib?" Giana repeated, pushing herself up to sit, tucking the blanket around her nude body. She tried to ignore the flash of excitement that flared inside her at that idea to focus on logic. "I won't be comfortable in that."

"Not a baby crib, Flame. A little girl crib. I ordered a light oak one with pink upholstered crowns at each end."

"Really? Like my old headboard?" Her queen-size headboard from her apartment hadn't fit Koa's king-size bed. They'd stored it in his basement. Koa thought the team could modify it somehow.

"As close as I could get to it. I think I remember oak is the same type of wood as your bedroom furniture."

"It is." She studied his face to make sure he wasn't messing with her. "Really? You ordered a little girl crib?"

"And some other things. I thought I might let you choose your bedding. Want to come sit with Daddy and tell me what you like?"

Giana nodded eagerly. "Nothing scratchy."

"Of course not." Koa tugged her cover away, pulling it gently from her hands. "Daddy loves your body, Giana. You don't need to hide from me."

She opened her mouth to protest and snapped it shut. He'd definitely seen her from all angles. "Could I have a T-shirt to wear? You know, just so I don't get cold?"

"I'll get you something to wear while you go potty." Koa rescued Jelly and Tiger before the stuffies could tumble to the floor as she scrambled out of bed at that reminder.

"I'll be right back," Giana promised and scurried from the room. When she glanced back to see if he was watching, his gaze focused on her bottom. His half-smile reassured her he enjoyed looking at her.

When she came back, Koa had spread a towel out on the bed. Next to it was a cute basket decorated like a bunny, complete with ears and a tail. She walked closer, saying, "That's adorable, Daddy. What's it for?"

"The bunny holds all sorts of supplies for me to take care of you, little girl. Eventually, he'll sit on your changing table."

"Changing table? To change what?" Her gaze landed on the poufy object on the other side of the basket. "What's that?"

"Come here, little girl. You had a tough day. Daddy's going to take special care of you for a while. Bottles, diapers, everything a little girl needs to let the outside world drift away."

"I'm okay, Daddy. I don't need that stuff."

"We'll try everything to find out what your heart needs.

Even if your brain panics a bit. Let Daddy show you, and then you can use your safeword if it doesn't work for you. You slept very well after drinking your bottle."

"It was yummy," she had to admit.

"I'm glad. Come here, Flame." Koa wrapped his hands around her waist. After lifting her, he stretched her out on the towel and immediately lifted her legs high into the air.

She expected him to tuck the diaper underneath her, but Koa picked up a small tube and snapped off the end. He pressed her legs forward, parting them and exposing her small entrance between her buttocks. When she struggled at being exposed so intimately, Koa simply lifted her legs higher, controlling her movements.

"Be good, Flame. Daddy's going to check your temperature. You'll get used to me paying attention to your cute bottom." He pressed the open tube against her tight rosette. A cool substance covered her entrance before he pushed the tube inside and injected the rest of that substance.

"What's that?"

"Lubricant. It will make the thermometer slide into your bottom easily." He set the empty tube down on the towel by her hip and pressed his finger into her bottom.

Giana gasped at the intrusion and tried to ignore the shivery thrills that raced through her at his intimate caretaking. "Daddy, no!"

"You'll get used to Daddy's touch here, little girl. You are very tight. I'll need to prepare you to take my cock here."

She swallowed hard. Somewhere inside, Giana understood he would not allow her to hide her desires and interests. She'd always been curious, but hadn't ever trusted anyone enough to admit that.

He withdrew his finger and wiped away the slick material on a tissue before grabbing a thick thermometer from the basket. Before she could react, he pressed the tip to her tight entrance and pushed it deep inside. The lubricant foiled her attempts to clench her muscles to stop it.

"Don't be naughty. Your diaper's elastic will feel scratchy on thoroughly spanked skin."

"Daddy! Take it out!"

"Ten minutes." He twirled it gently between his fingers, drawing all her attention to this previously forbidden spot.

"I don't like this," she whined.

"Lying to Daddy is not a great idea. Little girls need lots of care to keep them healthy and happy. Perhaps I need to place something in your bottom frequently to help you adjust to having my touch here."

She shook her head quickly, hoping to push that thought out of his mind. His answering, "Hmmm!" told her she hadn't distracted him from that idea. The swirling thermometer slid a bit deeper into her bottom.

The feeling that he was in total control soothed her. The tension in her body eased, and she relaxed on the bed.

"That's my good girl," he praised her. Koa draped her legs over his broad shoulder and grabbed an object from the tangle of covers. "I wondered where your pacifier went. You were too tired to see it earlier. Cute, isn't it?"

Gianna smiled and reached for the pacifier eagerly. The outside was decorated like a bunny's mouth with a pink nose and white teeth. It must make her look like a bunny when she sucked on it. Popping it into her mouth, she sucked happily on the soft bulb.

"You are adorable, Flame."

The pacifier made the time fly by faster. She glanced up immediately at her daddy when he slid the thermometer from her. He turned the thick tube to check the results.

"Your temperature is perfect, little girl. Let's get you wrapped up so Daddy will leave your cute bottom alone and fill your tummy instead."

She sucked furiously on her pacifier, glad she didn't have to respond to that. After cleaning up the thermometer and putting it away, her daddy set her feet wide apart on the bed. He stopped her automatic move to pull her knees together and shook his head at her.

"Sorry," she mumbled through the pacifier.

"Daddy doesn't mind reminding you, Flame."

He efficiently unfolded the diaper and tucked it under her hips. As he wrapped it around her body, she wondered how many times he'd done this.

"That wasn't a good thought, little girl." Koa popped the pacifier from her lips. "What's going on in your mind?"

"You're good at that."

"And that's a bad thing? We don't want your diaper to fall off."

"How many little girls have you put diapers on?" she demanded.

"Remember that I was the older brother…"

"Oh!" Immediately, she felt embarrassed.

"Always tell me if you're upset by something. It's better that we talk about something immediately than to stew about it. Will you promise to let me know if something bothers you?"

"Can I promise I'll try?" she asked.

"Thank you, little girl. Now, let's get you up! Do you want to keep your pacifier, or shall we put that back in the bunny basket?"

Giana looked at the pacifier in her hand and hesitated. She really didn't want to give it back. Slowly, she held it out to him.

"You can keep it, Flame." He laughed as she immediately popped it back into her mouth. "I'm glad you like it. Would you like to bring Jelly and Tiger into the dining room? I'll put these things away until we need them again."

When he set the basket on the dresser, she wondered, "How quickly will he need those things?" It must be soon. The basket was literally the only thing on his dresser in his military-tidy house.

"Oops!" she gasped as he lifted her off the bed and set her feet on the floor. "Thanks."

"You're welcome."

He held on to her as she regained her balance. The padding between her legs created a slight challenge. When he released her waist to take her hand, she shifted her stuffies to one arm and clung to him for stability. Her daddy walked slowly with her down the hallway. The rocking steps made her feel littler than ever before.

After escorting her to the table, Koa helped her sit down. The diaper bunched under her bottom. It was a constant reminder that she could be little here. Giana played happily with her stuffies as he brought everything to the table.

"That's everything," he announced, setting the last dish down.

"Daddy. I can't eat without a shirt," she told him seriously. Her mother had always required her brother and dad to be fully covered at the table.

"I've got you, Flame." He gently tugged a towel-like item with a circle opening in the middle over her head. It draped over her chest and back, concealing her skin.

She ran her hand over the fabric and smiled. It was soft and fluffy against her skin. "I like this."

"I'm glad." Koa dropped a kiss on the top of her head. He plucked her stuffies from her hands and drew another chair close to her for her friends before sitting down.

He filled a divided plate for her that kept all her food from touching. He even stopped and cut her chicken into bite-size pieces before setting it in front of her. "Eat, Flame. I know you're hungry."

Giana picked up her fork immediately and stabbed a piece of the diced fruit. Popping it into her mouth, she discovered it was a piece of apple, not the pear she'd expected. "This isn't from a can, is it?" she mumbled as she crunched the tidbit.

"Don't talk with your mouth full, little girl. And, yes. It is fresh. I won't eat that mushy processed stuff. Do you like it?"

She swallowed carefully and answered, "It's yummy. And you put all sorts of fruit in here. Look. Here's a pear. I thought that's what I put in my mouth."

Poking around at the fruit salad as she chewed her newest find, Giana scrunched her nose up. A cherry. She didn't like cherries. Did she have to eat it?

"You don't like those?" he guessed.

Giana shook her head and answered, "Not at all."

"Perfect. More for me. Want to feed me that one and I'll avoid dishing anymore up for you?"

Happily, Giana stabbed the offending fruit and held it out to her daddy. He made everything so much better. As he playfully gobbled it off her fork, her heart skipped a beat. She'd never cared this much about anyone. She loved him.

Smiling down at her plate, she took a second to savor that realization. She loved Koa.

"Are you okay, Flame?" he asked, covering her hand with his.

"The absolute best I've ever been. Thank you, Daddy, for saving me from the red yucky monster."

"Any time, little girl. Any time."

CHAPTER 13

By the time she finished work the next day, Giana felt awful. The scratchy throat she'd attributed to the smoke from yesterday's major fire had gotten worse as the day progressed. Now each time she swallowed, her throat felt like broken glass. Her hoarse cough wasn't helping it.

"Captain, you don't sound good," Tom said from her doorway.

"I'm fine," she assured the firefighter who frequently wanted to hang out in her office.

"Maybe you should go to the doctor. I could take you," he offered, coming in to sit in the chair in front of her desk.

"I'm busy, Tom. I can't stop to talk," she croaked. "Go check on the supplies in the medical cabinet." She'd already asked him twice to do the inventory. The job would take several hours and keep the man out of her hair for the rest of her shift. He couldn't be done.

"The other guys can do it. I've been trying to talk to you all day," Tom said, appearing peeved.

"Emergency?" she snapped.

"Well, no. I thought we needed to get to know each other better. I'd love to take you…"

"I don't date firefighters, Tom. I've told you this before. If you ask me one more time, I'm going to write you up for harassment. No means no."

"Women change their minds all the time. I think we'd be a good match. You just have to give me a chance."

Giana straightened her spine and shot him a stern look. "Get out of my office. Pack your things and report to station four within the hour. That will be your new home base effective immediately."

"You can't do that!"

She stared at him. When Tom didn't leave, she glanced at her watch. "You're down to fifty-seven minutes before you're considered late for your shift at station four."

Tom glared at her, holding her gaze to challenge her authority. Giana didn't address him again. She turned to pick up her phone and called the fire captain at his new station.

"Good news, Robert. I'm permanently transferring an employee to station four." Ignoring Tom, she listened to the other captain's response. "I noticed this morning in the district meeting that you were down two firefighters while we had one extra. That should help balance out the numbers."

After disconnecting, Giana focused back on the computer screen. She continued to fill out the state reports that tortured her every month as the worst part of her job and completely ignored the clueless firefighter who had just become someone else's problem. The creak of his chair a few minutes later clued her in that he was still in her office.

Giana glanced at her wrist and then met his gaze. "Leave, Tom."

"You're making a big mistake."

"Take advantage of this fresh start. Station four is your last chance," she told him bluntly.

"You fuck…" Tom bit off his words. Smashing his hands down on the armrests of the chair, he rocketed toward her.

Giana didn't flinch or move away. She said one word, "Camera." That stopped him in his tracks.

"You're recording me?"

"Yes. I don't do the 'he said, she said' thing." Giana looked past Tom to the older firefighter hovering outside her office. Mark had stopped immediately, shocked by Tom's aggressive lean over her desk.

"Mark, Tom is going to station four. Could you help him collect his belongings? He will not be returning here," Giana told him in a crisp, authoritarian tone.

"You got it, Captain," Mark answered.

Tom whirled and swore under his breath to see that they had an audience. Turning back at Giana, he growled, "This is bullshit."

"Watch where you step on the way out," she told him evenly.

"Come on, Tom. You're not accomplishing anything here," Mark said.

Shaking with anger, Tom allowed himself to be ushered out of her space. As soon as he was out of sight, Giana accessed the camera feed she'd installed in her office. She copied it into Tom's station file and saved it.

A few minutes later, Mark appeared at her door. "He's gone. Are you okay?"

"Perfect. I appreciate your backup, Mark. Was there a reason you'd come to talk to me?"

"Can I get a personal day scheduled? The doctors have scheduled my daughter to have her C-section next month."

"Of course. Congratulations. Send me the date. I'll make

sure the duty roster gives you a couple of days off to enjoy your next grandson," Giana assured him.

"Thanks, Captain. And I'm sorry."

"For taking time off with your family?" she asked.

"For the total ass. The entire station will be glad he's gone. Tom is toxic."

"You hadn't said anything," Giana said.

"I figured he'd hang himself soon."

"That he did. Clue me in next time if someone is disrupting the peace around here if I don't pick up on it," Giana requested.

"Will do, Captain. Be careful. He's angry."

"Always. Thank you, Mark." Giana turned back to her paperwork. She wouldn't give Tom another moment of her time. She had a drink of her now-cold coffee and grimaced. Too bad she didn't have time to make a coffee run.

GIANA PULLED the jacket closer around her neck. How cold had someone cranked the air conditioner up? This was ridiculous.

She reviewed the document on her screen one more time before copying it to her supervisor and pressing submit. Using the last of her energy, she pushed herself up from her chair and headed for the kitchen to return her coffee cup.

As she walked in, the firefighters on that shift greeted her eagerly. One female clapped, and the others joined in. Giana froze. Her worn-out brain took a second to realize they were celebrating Tom's transfer. Unable to discuss personnel issues with other employees, she changed the subject.

"Did I actually tear out all my hair over this month's reports?" she croaked.

Several smoothed over the right side of their hair,

signaling to her that she'd definitely rucked up her normally restrained bun. Giana didn't even care. "I'm off for a couple days. Stay safe, everyone."

"Thanks, Captain," came from all sides.

The woman who'd started the clapping suggested, "Go to the doctor, Captain. You sound awful."

"Thanks, Liz. I'll definitely consider that." Giana nodded her thanks and headed for the door.

The trip to her truck exhausted the last of her energy. Giana dragged herself into the driver's seat and pulled her seatbelt around her. She dropped her forehead onto the steering wheel. The blare of her phone made her wince. Surely this wasn't an emergency. She hadn't even gotten out of the parking lot.

Daddy appeared on her screen as the caller. Giana fumbled with the phone. "Hi, Daddy. I'm on my way home."

"What's up with your voice?" he asked.

"I'm sure it's from the smoke yesterday."

"Does your throat hurt?"

"Yeah. I feel like a truck hit me. Maybe I'm coming down with something. I've been so cold today. I think the air conditioning at the station must be broken."

"You're not running a fever, are you?"

She could hear the concern in his voice. The memory of him taking her temperature the little girl way made Giana shiver. "I need some sleep, and I'll be better."

"Drive home safely, little girl."

Giana could tell from his voice that the conversation wasn't over. He was worried about her. And Koa worried meant he was in full Daddy mode. She smiled to herself and thought, "Not like he's ever out of Daddy mode."

Navigating the busy streets was torture on a good day. This evening, it was a lot for her to handle. She'd never been so happy to see a house in her whole life as when she pulled into her daddy's driveway. Giana dropped her forehead back onto the steering wheel to rest.

A knock on her window made her look up. Koa stood outside, concern etched on his handsome face. "Little girl. Unlock the door for me."

She ran her fingers over the buttons, trying to process which one worked. Finally, she heard the whir of the motor as the lock released. Her daddy opened the door and stepped close. He pressed a hand to her forehead and shook his head.

"You are burning up, Flame. Why didn't you tell me you were this ill? I would have picked you up."

"I just need some sleep," she mumbled and struggled to get out of the seat.

"Let me help you, baby." Koa quickly unfastened her seatbelt to free her.

Giana melted into his arms as he picked her up. Resting her heavy head on his shoulder, she closed her eyes. Trusting Koa to take care of her was so easy. She had vague impressions of being carried into the house and settled on top of their bed. Curling onto her side around her stuffies, Giana crashed into sleep.

CHAPTER 14

"Zale?" Koa spoke quietly into his phone. He could hear Pippa talking in the background.

"Koa? Is everything okay?"

"I'm sorry to interrupt your free time. Could you come check on Giana?"

"I'm okay," Giana croaked.

Her rough and weak voice wouldn't have carried through to the medic. Koa leveled a hard look on her and she relaxed back on the covers. She hadn't struggled at all when he'd taken her temperature. That told him everything. His little girl was sick.

Zale's voice refocused him. "I'll be right over. Give me an idea of what we're dealing with so I can bring some medicine in case she needs it."

"Sore throat, fever, exhaustion," Koa listed his concerns.

"Got it. A lot of strep throat is going around. I'll bring a test. Give me ten minutes and I'll be there," Zale promised.

"Thank you, Zale. I'll owe you," Koa told him, grateful for his help. Zale had patched him up a dozen times on missions.

He trusted the skilled medic with his own life. Zale would take care of Giana.

"I don't want to see a doctor," Giana grumbled in her hoarse voice.

"Good. You'll get to see Zale. Drink some juice, Flame. We need to keep you hydrated."

"I'm tired of drinking," she said.

Koa watched her lips thin as she pressed her lips together tightly. "Sick little girls who misbehave can still earn consequences."

She wrinkled her nose at him. Koa steeled himself to not react to her cuteness. He held the sippy glass to her lips. "Drink, Giana. You'll feel better."

After snorting her disapproval, Giana relented and drank the mixture from the cup. "Mmm," she hummed in enjoyment.

"I thought you'd like that," Koa said. "You can trust me, little girl."

She nodded and handed the cup back. "Tired, Daddy. I'm going back to sleep."

"Rest, little girl."

A few minutes later, Koa ran quietly through the house to open the door for Zale who carried a box of supplies. "Hey, Zale. I'm glad you're here."

"Let's go see that little girl of yours," Zale suggested.

"She's in bed." Koa led the way to their room. "Giana? Zale is here."

"No shots," she said, before coughing.

"That's a nasty cough, Giana. Would you like me to see if I can help you?" Zale asked.

"I don't want to make Pippa angry. She's my friend," Giana whispered.

"Pippa sent you this picture," Zale said, walking forward to hand Giana a piece of paper. He waited as she fumbled with the covers to get a hand free to take it. Koa stepped closer to see a decorated, coloring book page showing a bunny with an ice pack on his head. Underneath, Pippa had carefully printed, *Let Daddy help you.*

* * *

WHEN GIANA GLANCED up at him, Zale said, "It's your choice, little girl. I'm glad to examine you and help you feel better, but I will treat you as a little girl. If you're not comfortable with that, I'll be glad to suggest a great doctor who treats adults if you don't currently have a physician."

Giana was quiet for a few seconds. Zale would treat her as intimately as her own daddy did. Pippa had told her before that Pippa understood Zale would see others naked to take care of them. Giana had seen how much Zale cared for Pippa. She understood Zale's intention was simply to do as he stated—to help her feel better.

"I feel awful, Zale. Everybody trusts you. Please help me."

"You got it, Giana." Zale turned to Koa and asked, "Would you undress Giana completely so I can examine her while I get myself organized?"

"You've got it." Koa brushed his fingers through Giana's hair before leaning down to kiss her forehead. "Let's get you feeling better, Flame."

When she nodded, he gently turned back the blanket he'd thrown over her earlier. He helped her sit up and stripped off the uniform shirt she still wore from work and her nononsense bra. Giana settled back against the covers with a sigh of relief when that small expenditure of energy challenged her. She could see the concern wrinkling Koa's face when she was so weak.

"Zale's going to help you, little girl. Let's get these pants off you." When she tried to help, Koa gently tugged her hands away and finished removing her clothing.

"Roll Giana onto her side, facing the middle of the bed," Zale directed, picking up the thick thermometer case.

Koa moved her into position with her knees bent up toward her tummy.

Giana tried to roll backward. Koa stood by her side, holding her in position. "Be good, little girl."

"I'm going to check your temperature first, Giana. Relax your bottom," Zale instructed, gently parting her buttocks with a gloved hand.

Cool air flowed over her small entrance for a split second before Zale's finger applied lubricant to the tight ring of muscles. Giana groaned when he pressed that digit inside and rubbed the mixture on the sides of the narrow passage. Despite Koa's frequent attentions here as he cared for her and during their sexy times, the touch felt taboo and arousing. She could feel herself getting wet. Both men would see.

Koa's hand caressed her shoulder as Zale's finger slid from her bottom. "What a perfect little girl you are, Flame."

She knew what was coming next. The thick thermometer filled her. She shivered at the feel of the cold glass invading her. Koa quickly subdued her move to straighten her legs and roll away.

"Behave, Flame. I will spank you if you're naughty," Koa warned.

Giana froze immediately. She'd quickly learned that Koa always told the truth. He wouldn't threaten anything that he didn't intend to follow through on. Time seemed to creep by as the thick device in her bottom warmed. Finally, Zale removed it from her bottom.

"That's too high, Giana. No wonder you don't feel good," Zale commiserated with her.

Zale tucked something under her hips before Koa rolled her onto her back. It crinkled under her weight.

"Let's sit her up, Koa. Why don't you prop her up from behind?" Zale suggested as they lifted her torso from the covers.

The bed dipped behind her as Koa propped one knee on the mattress. He helped her settle back against him. Zale smiled at Giana as she met his gaze. Somehow, looking directly at him felt more intimate. Giana crossed her arms over her chest.

Zale gently pressed her hands down to her sides. "None of that, little girl. I need to see all of you to help you feel better. Okay?"

That slight effort had wiped out the last of her energy. Giana nodded and whispered, "Okay."

"Good girl. Can you open your mouth for me, Giana? It sounds like a frog is living in your throat," Zale teased.

Obediently, Giana followed his directions and let Zale examine her. The feel of the tongue depressor was familiar and reassuring. Zale knew what he was doing. The thought that his use of the wooden stick proved his medical knowledge tickled Giana. Unfortunately, that started her coughing.

"Yep, you've got it, Giana," Zale said sadly.

"What?" she whispered.

"The crud," he said seriously before winking at her.

"I knew it," Koa joked from behind her.

Giana rolled her eyes. They were such daddies, trying to distract her from feeling so bad.

"I'm going to check your ears and nose, Giana, but I suspect you've caught the strep throat going around. I need to swab inside a bit. I'll try to be quick. Try not to cough if you can."

Zale opened a tube and quickly brushed the tip of the swab over the sore spots in her throat. Giana struggled not to cough, but it was so hard. Thankfully, Zale was an expert at getting a quick sample.

"That's it, Giana. You can cough now," he assured her as he sealed the collector inside the tube and labeled it. "Koa, help her take a drink."

"That..." *cough, cough, cough,* "was mean," Giana accused, sending him a mean look.

"Be nice to Zale, Flame. He has a tough job having to do things he knows you won't like, but that need to be done," Koa reminded her as he held a cup to her lips.

Giana relented slightly. "Okay."

"I'm going to listen to your heart and lungs next," Zale told her. He handled the responsibility and her criticism easily. She guessed he was used to it.

"Take a deep breath for me, Giana," Zale instructed, pressing the bell of his stethoscope against her chest.

"C-cold," Giana protested at the feel of the metal circle on her skin. Her nipples contracted into tight buds as she rounded her shoulders forward.

"Sorry, little girl." Zale removed the cold bell and rubbed it on his T-shirt.

When he pressed it back to her skin, Giana sighed in relief. "Better."

She held still this time as he listened carefully to her chest. Giana rested heavily against Koa's supporting frame. She hated that simply sitting up sapped all her energy.

Zale sat back and removed the earpieces of his stethoscope. "Okay, little girl. I think I have enough information to help you feel better. Your daddy can help you stretch out."

He turned his attention to Koa. "I'll run the strep test to make sure, but I'm fairly sure that's what she has picked up. I'm going to give her a broad-spectrum antibiotic to combat several strains of bugs. She should be better by the time the results come back. If not, that will give us the information we need to tailor her treatment more specifically."

Giana let out a long-suffering sigh and sent good vibes toward Pippa for sharing her skilled daddy to help her. This was awful.

"Thanks, Zale. I hate to see her like this," Koa said, brushing the hair from her eyes.

"I'll give her a shot…"

"No needles!" Giana rallied to protest. She hated injections.

Zale looked at her sternly and continued, "Shot first to jump-start the healing process and then we'll put some medicine in her bottom to melt and absorb."

"Not in my bottom!" Giana wailed. This was awful.

"Your daddy will take care of everything for you," Zale told her firmly before glancing at Koa. "The medicine will be most effective if you press it as deep as possible into her rectum. If Giana is naughty and tries to push it out, hold your finger in place until the suppository melts and then rub the mixture around thoroughly. Contractions from an orgasm or two will draw the medicine deeper into her system."

Giana glanced at her daddy. They weren't talking about this, were they?

"Got it. No sex until she feels better?" Koa asked.

"No. That will tax her breath. Let's get the infection cleared up, and then Giana can resume all her normal activities. I do not want her to go to work until her temperature has registered at normal for twenty-four hours."

"I have to go to work if there's an emergency," Giana muttered.

"Other captains can fill in for you," Koa said confidently.

Giana shrugged and wondered how he knew so much. "I'll get better fast," she promised.

"Let's get that process started. Your daddy will help you roll over on your side," Zale said. He stood to rustle through his supplies.

After getting her into position, Koa blocked her view as Zale prepared the injection. Giana jumped at the feel of the cold disinfecting swab. She squeezed her eyes closed and clenched her jaw to prepare for the pain.

"Pinch her nipple, Koa," Zale instructed.

Giana blinked her eyes open wide at that request. She opened her mouth to protest and gasped. "Ouch!" A small sting on her bottom followed as she recovered from Koa's touch.

"Shot done," Zale announced as he dealt with the syringe.

In shock, she looked at him. "You gave it to me? That was nothing but a tiny pinch."

"All done. You did very well with your daddy's help. He's a medic's best resource," Zale told her. "Alright, Koa, I'm going to have you administer her suppositories. Gloves?"

"No, thanks," Koa waved them off.

"Alright. Two suppositories placed deep. Hold in place if she struggles. Add an orgasm or two," Zale reminded him.

Giana hoped the bed would open up and swallow her. Zale was going to watch Koa insert the medicine? And then help her orgasm?

Koa got straight to work. He coated the tip of the medicine with lubricant and pressed it deep. Giana tightened all her muscles in vain as he easily pushed the bullet-shaped dose into her bottom. A second one followed quickly, and Koa held his finger in place.

"Be a good girl, Giana. The medicine needs to stay inside you," Koa said sternly.

She could feel the intruders inside her. They were cool inside her warm bottom. Koa's thick finger filled her, making it impossible to push them out. A fuzzy feeling gathered inside her. "Daddy…" she said and yawned widely.

"The medicine will have a drowsy effect. That will help her sleep," Zale explained.

"It absorbs quickly," Koa said.

"It's extremely effective. Can I hand you a vibrator?" Zale asked.

"Please. There's one in that drawer." He nodded to the drawer where he kept all the toys. Giana closed her eyes as Zale retrieved the device, knowing the medic would see everything.

A buzz sounded close. Giana didn't open her eyelids. She could hear Zale gathering all his supplies. Koa pushed her bent legs higher and ran the tip of the vibrator over her outer lips.

Examined, probed, and turned on by having two men watching her, Giana tried not to respond. Her body had different intentions. As he pressed the wand through her pink folds, Giana exploded into a massive orgasm. A second and third followed quickly. She felt herself squirt as the sensations overwhelmed her and she blacked out.

CHAPTER 15

Koa pulled into his driveway with a smile. He had time to take a shower and whip up some dinner before his little girl arrived home from her shift. Giana had needed four days at home to recover from her illness. While she'd rebelled against his insistence that she be fever-free for twenty-four hours as Zale had required, Giana had texted her appreciation today that she hadn't passed it along to her staff when three firefighters had called in sick after another returned too quickly. The illness was rampant this year, as Zale had reported.

It had taken a couple of weeks for them to settle comfortably into each other's schedules. Thank goodness, they both understood that work could have emergencies. Their career requirements fit well together. Either of them could be called to duty at a moment's notice.

He'd always looked forward to the next time they'd get to see each other. Giana had adapted well to shrugging off her responsibilities from work when she walked through the front door. It helped that he made a point of greeting her with a kiss and a cuddle before taking her to her new nursery to strip off her adult clothes. Dressed in cute, comfortable clothing like a swishy dress or leggings and a T-shirt, Giana normally didn't fret over job worries.

Sometimes, she needed extra attention to flip that switch from 'responsible for everything' to 'little girl' mode. A red bottom was usually his last resort when she got stuck in work mode. Thank goodness changing clothes, hugging her stuffies, and her daddy's affection usually did the trick to help Giana shrug off her work concerns. Those sweet interventions saved her from too many spankings.

Koa showered and pulled on a pair of shorts. He had pulled out the ingredients for a Greek salad he'd planned for dinner with chicken when a knock sounded on the door.

"Did you forget your key, Flame?" he called as he walked to the door. Funny. She didn't answer him.

"The door is open," he said as he twisted the knob.

"Good to know. Should I just walk in next time?" his neighbor three houses down asked.

"Oh. Hi, Sharon. Let me go get a shirt. I was expecting Giana."

"No need on my behalf. I'll be glad to check out the scenery."

"I'll get a shirt. One minute, please."

Koa hadn't liked Sharon the first time they'd met. Her husband was an officer on base, but as a pilot, he traveled a lot. His wife flirted with everyone. He suspected Sharon's activities weren't limited only to talking while her husband flew.

Koa jogged to his bedroom and grabbed a T-shirt. He stopped in the hall to pull it on before reappearing at the entrance where she could see. To his surprise when he reached the open family room and kitchen area, Sharon stood inside with the door closed.

When he stopped in his tracks to look at her incredulously, Sharon said, "It was getting hot out there. I didn't think you'd mind?"

"Sorry, Sharon. I think it's better if we step outside."

Koa didn't wait for her to answer, but brushed by her to grab the doorknob. Sharon stepped forward into his path and crumpled dramatically to the floor when he couldn't avoid brushing against her.

"Ouch! I've turned my ankle. Could I have some ice, please? I think I'm supposed to put it up, aren't I?" she asked with a grimace, clutching her left foot.

"Let's get you back to your house, and you can take it easy for the rest of the night," Koa suggested, wishing to get her out of his house as soon as possible.

Koa lifted her to her feet and left her standing by the couch as he opened the door. Sharon took one limping step and shook her head. "I can't do it. I'll take a seat and rest my ankle for a bit. I'm sure it will be fine in a few minutes."

Trying to think quickly, Koa searched for a way to transport her a few houses down the street. He didn't have a wheelchair to push her in. Getting her into the truck would take as much time as walking down the street.

Mentally shaking her head, he offered, "If you'll allow me, I'll carry you back to your house."

"If you don't mind putting those big muscles to use…" Her voice trailed off.

The last thing Koa wanted to do was get close to her, much less touch Sharon. Trying to keep his face from revealing his true feelings toward her, Koa pasted a smile on his face. He scooped Sharon off her feet and walked out the door. *Crap!*

"Hi?" Giana appeared exhausted and totally shocked to see him carrying another woman.

"Hi, neighbor. Just borrowing Koa's brute strength. I'll

send him home soon." Sharon ran her fingers over Koa's bulging biceps. "Maybe?"

"Keep him," Giana told the flirtatious woman.

She circled around them and headed into the house as Koa said, "Giana, she hurt her…" The door crashing closed behind Giana interrupted his explanation.

"Oops! She seemed angry. Trouble in paradise?" Sharon asked, looking too pleased.

"I'll get you to your porch, then you're on your own," Koa told Sharon, walking as fast as possible.

"Whoa! Slow down. You're jarring my ankle." Sharon lifted her right foot as if to remind him she was wounded.

Koa stopped and set Sharon on her feet in the middle of the sidewalk. "It's your right foot now? That's telling. You supposedly hurt your left foot when you entered my house without permission. Make your own way home. Don't bother me again." He turned and immediately ran back to his house.

"Koa! I hurt myself at your home. I could sue you. At least get me home," Sharon shouted after him.

Koa ignored her and raced up his driveway. Sharon definitely knew how to put on a show for the neighbors. As he got to the front door, it opened, and Giana stepped out with her work uniforms clutched in one hand and a plastic bag in the other. He was sure it contained her stuffies.

"Giana, she faked an injury, and carrying her was the only way I could get her out of here," Koa explained.

"I wondered how long it would take until you were tired of playing Daddy."

Her expression broke his heart. He had to get her to listen to him. Koa stepped forward and wrapped his arms around her. Instantly, Giana struggled. She was in amazing physical shape and a handful to control, but Koa wouldn't let her go.

Picking her off the ground, he hauled her kicking and

yelling into his house. He slammed the door closed with his elbow and set her feet on the floor. "Stop and listen. I'll let you leave in a few minutes if you still want to."

"You're damn right I want to leave. Probably every housewife in the neighborhood is calling the police right now." Giana glared at him.

"I got home and took a shower. Like I usually do, I put on shorts and started dinner. Sharon came here for some reason. I still don't know why."

"Looks like she got swept off her feet by your charm." Giana spat the words at him.

"When I answered the door, she leered at my chest, making me very uncomfortable. I didn't want to encourage her, so I excused myself to get a shirt. When I came back, she had waltzed inside."

"You didn't want to encourage her?"

He bristled at her tone. "I did not invite her attention, nor have I given her any indication in the year that I've lived here that I was interested in her."

"Right. So how did she end up in your arms?" Giana crossed her own over her chest.

"She faked falling and then pretended to have damaged her ankle."

"And how do you know she made her injury up?"

"I left her standing in the middle of the sidewalk when she forgot which side she'd supposedly hurt—first it was her left ankle and then her right." Koa fumed. He'd never decked a woman and would never do so, but Sharon had earned a lot of bad karma through this farce.

"You really don't want her?"

"Not a chance in hell that I would ever touch that woman —even if my life hinged on it. And I'm not tired of playing Daddy. That's who I am." Koa held Giana's gaze with his. He needed to know she understood.

Giana dropped the hangers in her hand and hugged her stuffies closer. "I really screwed this up, didn't I?"

"No. That bitch screwed this up. She's not happy in her marriage, so she had to make sure everyone else is as miserable as she is," Koa said bluntly. He stepped forward and pulled Giana close. He squeezed her until she squeaked.

"Are you going to spank me?"

"For getting upset?" he asked, taking a step back to study her face. "I'm glad you cared enough about us to get upset."

"I should have listened to you."

"Yes, you should have. And I should have checked the peephole and never answered that door. I'm putting in a ring camera tomorrow after training."

"Surely, she'll never come back," Giana said.

"Her type never stops. I'd talk to her husband when he returns, but I don't think that will make a difference."

A sound made him stop and look around. "Do you hear music?"

"Oh! That's my phone."

Giana fumbled to pull it out of her back pocket. "Hello?"

"Someone broke into my apartment?" she asked a few seconds later and then finally, "I'll be right there."

After disconnecting from the call, Giana explained, "That was my apartment complex. My neighbors reported that someone vandalized my apartment. The police need me to come and tell them if anything is missing."

Her hands shook slightly as her gaze darted around. He knew her brain whirled around in her head. "I'll drive."

"You'll come with me?"

"You'd have to shackle me somewhere in the house to keep me here," he assured her. "Let me grab my keys."

She was already out the door when he caught up with her. "My truck," Koa said, steering her to the passenger seat.

He drove quickly but safely. Koa didn't make small talk.

He reached for her hand and held it, stopping the twisting movement in her lap. Giana immediately wrapped her other hand around his as well. He gave her fingers a gentle squeeze.

"We'll deal with whatever has happened."

She nodded and stared out the window as she clung to him.

When they pulled up to her building at the complex, Giana bailed out quickly. Koa turned off the engine and followed her. He didn't correct her for not waiting for him, but simply backed her up. When they reached the third floor, there were two police officers at the top of the stairs waiting for her.

"I'm Giana Mancini. What happened?"

"Your neighbor to the right called 911 when she got home from work. We found your door kicked in, and everything looked tossed around," the officer reported. "Your name and face are familiar. Do you work for the fire department?"

"I do. I'm the fire captain at station nine. Is Janet okay?" Giana asked.

"She's fine. The intruder was gone by the time she got home. We walked through without touching anything to ensure the place was empty."

"How bad is it?" Giana asked in a steady voice, but she reached for Koa's hand.

"I don't know if they were searching for something or focused on destruction. We need you to go check for anything missing or damaged. Make a list if you can. We'll add that to the report. When the culprit is caught, that information will affect the type of sentence he or she gets," one officer told her.

"Can my…" Giana paused.

"Partner. Can I go into the apartment with her?" Koa asked.

"I'd recommend that," the second officer readily agreed.

They stepped inside the door and could see the extent of the damage more clearly than from the outside. Koa walked past her a few feet and picked up a notepad on the floor next to the kitchen. Searching under a scattering of things obviously swept from the counter, he located a pen.

"Let me know what you see."

"A mess! Thank goodness I hadn't left much in the refrigerator." Giana pointed at the apple smashed into the wall. Someone had thrown that with force. And anger.

"Look at that!" She pointed to a potholder pinned to the wall with a butcher knife from the wooden block on the counter. The others were missing. "Who does something like this?"

Glancing around, Koa was sure this was personal. Not a normal theft. "Be careful where you step. There could be other hazards."

Giana shook her head and turned back into the living area. "The TV is smashed, as well as the lamps and my decorative vases. I had five on the shelves in here. I like… I liked the pretty glass."

"You still like it," Koa said, rubbing his hand over her shoulder. "Unfortunately, those are gone."

"That carpet is going to have to be replaced. Whoever this was, they ripped it. My deposit is so gone," Giana said sadly.

Another knife tethered a flap of cut flooring folded over to reveal the padding underneath. He couldn't spot any reason for that vandalism other than to cause damage—psychological warfare designed to scare his target. Koa knew that this was a man.

They quickly went through the rest of the house. In her bedroom, Giana gestured at the empty dresser drawers gaping open. "Thank goodness, we came last weekend and got the rest of my underwear and bras."

When she shivered, Koa knew she was thinking about the

vandal touching her private things. He wrapped his arm around her waist. "When we get out of here, I'm going to wrap you up in your blankie and hold you all night long. Focus for a few more minutes. Do you have any jewelry? Anything valuable?"

"Department store earrings at best. I don't have any place to wear diamonds." Her joke fell flat in the messy room. No fun could exist in this environment.

"Then I've got everything here. Let's go talk to the officers and see what happens next," Koa suggested.

As they walked back into the hallway, two maintenance guys appeared with a new door. "That answers one question," Koa pointed out before turning to the police. "Shall we move down here for a minute as they replace the door?"

"They made a real mess. I had already moved a bunch of stuff out so other than the TV, some decorative items, and the clothing they destroyed, there wasn't much left," Giana told the police.

"Thank you for being honest. Others would have made up a lot of mysterious, expensive items. Can you give me with a ballpark figure?" the lead officer asked.

"The TV was new and big. I think it cost eight hundred dollars. Add my glass vase collection and my clothes, the total is probably close to two thousand, twenty-five hundred," Giana suggested.

"That's what I would have estimated too. I'll put that in my report. Do you have insurance?" the other cop asked.

"I do."

"Call them in the morning. Don't clean until they see it. Get some estimates from the apartment management for repair costs. You may have to fight, but losing your apartment deposit should be included in the insurance amount."

"Thank you, Officers. I appreciate your help," Gianna told them.

Koa hated hearing the waver in her voice. He needed to get her home. The stress had wiped away the last of her energy.

"That guy took all those knives. That's not a good sign. Don't come here alone. We've seen a lot of home invasions. This one was personal," the officer warned.

With that, the police excused themselves and headed for their squad car. Koa looked at the men installing the door. They'd have it in place in a few minutes.

"Will you lock that and leave the keys at the office for us to pick up?" Koa asked.

"Yes, sir. You can pick up the keys there," one workman confirmed.

"Thanks." Koa ushered her out of the building and back to his truck. He opened the door for her to climb into the cab for the return trip.

She stopped and turned to face him. "I'm going to have to move. I can't live here ever again," Giana stated with more fire than he'd seen since they got here.

"Done. Are you off this weekend?"

"Yes."

"Then we move all your stuff out."

"It can't be that easy, Koa. Where am I going to move everything?" Her hands flailed through the air.

"Our basement," he answered without delay. To reassure her, he reached out to brush his hands over her shoulders and upper arms.

"Your basement?" she echoed, automatically correcting his statement.

"Our basement. This fits into my diabolical plan to have you with me."

"Koa, what if this doesn't work out?"

"That won't happen," he said. "I wanted to work on your nursery, anyway. When the guys help move you in, I can get them to help me set up a gym downstairs too. You're really helping me."

"You're not going to let me out of your sight after this, are you?"

Koa drew her close and hugged Giana tightly against him. "You're 100% right. Now, home?"

"Yes. Let's go home."

CHAPTER 16

From the safety of Koa's deck, Giana dealt with the problems weighing her down. Of course, everything had to be a huge hassle. Shaking her head in exasperation, Giana disconnected her call with the apartment complex management. They were doing all they could to help her, but she'd had to work through so many steps to resolve this issue: her contract, the deposit and unit damages, and the clean-up.

Koa's team had helped so much in clearing out the apartment. There had been little to salvage. Most of her furniture had been slashed. They'd simply set the couch and chairs down by the dumpster with a sign that they were free if someone wanted to reupholster them. Koa had hauled her mattress and box springs to the dumpster when they discovered the intruder had peed all over them.

Giana shuddered. That jerk had marked them like an animal. There was no way she'd ever sleep on those again.

The apartment had cameras scattered around the complex. They'd picked out footage of a non-resident entering her building, but his hat and bulky clothing had prevented the police from getting a clear picture to help in identifying the jerk. Giana had recognized his vehicle as the one belonging to the man who'd gotten so pissed at her for spacing out in the parking lot and for kissing Koa by his truck.

"You okay, Flame?" Koa asked, flipping burgers on the grill. "I still have those wings if you'd rather have those. I could throw them on, too."

"Sure, go ahead," she said offhand, not picking up on Koa's joke.

"Now I know something is wrong." He set down his spatula and walked toward her. "I figured hell would freeze over before the fire captain in you would okay me to cook poultry."

"I wish I'd gotten that guy's license plate number," she muttered.

"It was a stolen plate. I'm sure he's changed it by now."

"You ran it?"

"Not me. But a buddy."

"I asked in the apartment complex's Facebook group if anyone recognized that car. Several people thought they'd seen it, but no one knows who owns it," Giana told him.

"So, he doesn't live there but keeps showing up. Only one possible reason comes to my mind. He's watching someone in the complex. Combine that with his temper, I would bet it's a failed relationship."

"That's a lot of assumptions," Giana pointed out.

"But logical ones. I wonder if the police or apartment management would know who has a protective order in that area."

Giana shrugged her shoulders as her mind whirled. The man she'd had the unpleasant encounters with had a boiling temper. "Why would he have trashed my apartment?" She shivered at the thought that someone out of control had focused on her.

Koa was quickly at her side. Kneeling next to her chair, Koa pulled her into his arms to hug her close. "I know this is scary, Flame."

"The worst part is there's so much we don't know," she said and pushed against his hard chest to meet his concerned gaze.

"It's possible he has some mental problems, little girl. Or he's gotten you mixed up with someone else. Or he's pissed off about something totally different and has made you his target. Who knows?"

"Hopefully with me moved out, this will all go away."

"That would be incredible, but keep your guard up. A guy that angry doesn't give up easily," Koa warned.

"How could he find me?" Giana asked, trying to squelch that small voice in the back of her mind that had been working overtime to put her on edge.

"You have fire department emblems on your truck. Does it tell which station you're at?"

"Not anymore. I had those a few years ago, but random guys showed up at the station to ask me for a date. I advise all the female firefighters at my station to learn from my mistake."

"Smart. I'm glad you're looking out for others, but now, you need to focus on heeding your inner radar that tells you something is wrong. You call the police and then me immediately. We could get you one of those medallions that send out an alert."

"It's against policy, I can't. Not the warning device itself, but all jewelry is forbidden. The high-heat conditions would melt metal in a snap. No one wants jewelry embedding into their skin," Giana explained.

"Understandable. We have regulations as well."

An aroma wafted to her. "Um, Koa?" She waved a hand toward the grill.

"Fuck!" Koa jumped to his feet and raced back to the grill. He picked up one blackened hamburger patty. He tossed the meat onto a platter, where it landed with a hard thunk. Others followed as she tried not to laugh, covering her mouth with her hand.

He met her gaze before ruefully shaking his head. "You're not going to believe this, but I'm actually a grill master."

"Of course you are, Daddy," she said and then failed miserably at containing her giggles. Shaking his head, Koa joined her mirth. His deep laughter meshed perfectly with hers.

When she could talk, Giana said, "I really wanted pizza tonight, anyway. Take out?"

"I'll call," Koa muttered, pulling his phone out of his pocket.

Giana peeked up at Koa as he called her favorite Italian place. She didn't argue when he added vegetables to their pizza. She was getting really crafty at hiding them in her napkin.

He lifted an eyebrow when she smiled at that thought. Thank goodness he had to focus on the shopkeeper's questions. She lifted her shoulders and looked back at him as if she were completely innocent. Koa tilted his head, holding her gaze. Giana knew he was on to her and slumped back against her chair. She'd eat the vegetables. Tonight.

GIANA SCOPED out the parking lot as she drove into the apartment complex three days later. Her insurance and the managers had come to an agreement. They needed her to sign some papers, and the hassle would be over.

Laughing at herself for pulling her truck instinctively in her old parking spot, Giana slid out of the cab. "One last time for old times," she said to herself and headed to the complex office.

As she pulled the decorative door open, a woman with a hoodie pulled over her head approached on her way out. The woman froze in place and kept her head down. Fear radiated from her.

"Hi," Giana said cheerfully and stepped out of the doorway to allow her to leave.

"Sorry," the other woman mumbled and tucked a few strands of her long brown hair that had escaped back under the material before stepping outside.

Concerned, Giana watched her scan the area as the woman scurried to a shaded area by the brick exterior. She never raised her head to reveal her face. Giana got a brief glimpse of her profile.

Not wishing to stare, Giana stepped into the office and turned to make sure the swinging door had closed. She saw a movement a small distance away and focused on it automatically. To Giana's surprise, the mysterious woman walked into a building. The same building that Giana had vacated.

"Are you ready to be done with us, Giana?" a familiar voice called.

Giana turned to face the main section of the office and asked, "Who was that? She's not moving into my old apartment, is she?"

"Sorry, we don't reveal the names of our residents. It's strange you never ran into her. She's been here about six months."

"Oh. I guess if I worked regular, office-type hours I would have run into her at the mailboxes or something." Giana switched her focus back onto the matter at hand. "So, everything's set. I just need to pay the penalty for breaking my lease early?"

"The paperwork is all done. Take a second and look through these documents. And then, I need your signature at the bottom of the insurance settlement and on the early release from the rental agreement."

"Can I get a copy of these for my records?" Giana asked.

"This folder is yours." The manager handed her a manila envelope with photocopies.

"Thank you. I'll sit over there and read through everything. If I don't have any concerns, I'll sign and return it in a few minutes."

"Take all the time you need," the employee told her.

It took about ten minutes to read through all the fine print. The settlement with the insurance was very fair. Giana took a few minutes to compare various parts of the contract with her copy to make sure she had a good copy. It meshed perfectly.

With a flourish, Giana wrote her name on the spaces indicated by the bright arrow stickers, then she clicked the pen closed. *Thank goodness this is over.*

She returned the papers to the office manager with a smile. "Hey, thanks for all you've done to get this settled. I'm sorry this happened."

"Believe it or not, this isn't the worst thing I've seen while I've worked in the apartment biz. The most important thing is you're safe. Sometimes moving is the smartest thing to do, even if we're sorry to see you go."

"Thanks. Stay safe." As she walked out, Giana shook her head. She'd seen some tragic and frightening things in her line of work as well.

Movement near her old building caught her eye. Something familiar about that man tickled the back of her brain. He wore a souvenir-type bucket hat, pulled low over his face.

Giana didn't know why she got the impression its purpose wasn't to shield the sun from his eyes, but to conceal his face. As she watched, he turned to look at her truck for a few seconds too long.

Was he going to do something to her truck? He paced forward. When he'd gotten a couple of feet away from her truck, two kids and their mother burst from the next building. From the mother's unhappy scolding, Giana could tell the children had missed the bus.

When she turned back to see where the man was, the area around her truck was empty. Where had he gone? She should go back into the office and ask for security to walk her to her vehicle. But….

Long ago, Giana had learned to trust her instincts. They had kept her and her teams safe in many dangerous situations. Koa's punishment would be fierce if he ever found out she had acted impetuously.

The desire to get home made her shrug off her concerns. Silencing the warning signals going off in her brain, Giana continued toward her truck. She needed to get out of here and put this place behind her.

At the scrape of a boot on the pavement, Giana whirled around to see the man in the hat stand up from where he had crouched behind her vehicle. She balanced instinctively on the balls of her feet as she took a defensive posture. "What are you doing?"

"Picking up a quarter?" The man's tone was mocking and rough as he peered at her from under the brim of his hat. He held up the coin.

The feeling that she knew him grew stronger. She scanned his body. He was fit and powerful. The man put the money in his pocket. His hand brushed aside his baggy clothing showing a decoration on the skin at his waistline.

"Tom?" burst from her lips. She remembered when he'd

gotten that tattoo. The jerk had moaned about it for days as he attempted to walk around the fire station without a shirt to show it off. Giana had put a stop to that quickly.

His chin lifted, revealing his face. Tom's gaze radiated anger and something else that unsettled Giana.

"Did you trash my apartment?" she asked.

"Of course not. What apartment?" he said, shrugging. He visibly controlled his expression and smiled at her. "Do you live here or are you visiting someone?"

She needed to get out of here. Tom wasn't huge, but he was firefighter fit. Just by mass and male muscle power, he could overpower her. She almost liked the menacing look better than this smile. He made her skin crawl. He always had.

Giana ignored his question. "Hey, if you'll move away from my truck, I'll head to work. They're expecting me."

"You're not on the roster."

"I'm always on call." She waited for him to shift to a safer spot. He didn't.

"You're not going anywhere," he stated firmly. His menacing glare intensified. "I've tracked your truck for days and this is the first time you've been away from the fire station and that military hotshot."

She needed to get out of here now. *Think, Giana!*

CHAPTER 17

As her mind boggled at the thought he was tracking her, she knew better than to focus on that now. Pulling her bravado together, she told him, "I don't know what your game is here, but this isn't productive." Giana pulled out her phone to call for help. To distract him from her real intent, she added, "Let's plan a meeting for tomorrow during your shift. Put eight a.m. on your calendar."

"Put your phone away, Giana."

Ignoring his order, she held her phone up to unlock it with facial recognition. He grabbed the phone from her hand and slammed it to the pavement. "You never have understood your place, Captain." His voice had a snide, evil tone that added to the fear building inside her.

Stiffening her spine, she wouldn't allow him to see her fright. "Tom, we're going to move this conversation to the firehouse. Talking here isn't working."

"It's working fine for me. I think it's time you realized how little control you have. The days of you expecting everyone to jump when you order it are over. You know that three-fourths of the guys under your captaincy hope you'll get trapped under a burning beam in each fire."

Her stomach lurched at the hatred that coated every word and gesture Tom made. Controlling her expression was difficult; she did not want him to think he had scared her.

"Enough, Tom. Go get in your car and go home." Out of the corner of her eye, she calculated whether she could jump into her truck and slam the door before he got to her. There was no way. She'd have to think of something else.

Tom stepped forward, forcing her to step back until her back met the car in the next parking spot. Giana bumped it hard with her hip, hoping to set off an alarm. It simply rocked slightly.

He reached for her shoulder. Giana jerked away. She couldn't let him touch her.

"Stupid bitch. What makes you too good for me?"

"First off, I don't call anyone a stupid bitch. Second, I don't force myself on anyone. Good people don't do that."

Her head whipped back to avoid the open-handed slap he aimed at her. The pads of his fingers slammed into her cheek. Stinging pain lanced through her. Adrenaline flooded her body. Whatever he had planned, she would fight him every inch of the way.

A horn blared near the tailgate of her truck, startling them both. Taking advantage of Tom's distraction, Giana kicked him as hard as she could in the crotch. Tom shouted in pain and dropped to the ground, clutching himself as Giana ran away.

"I'm going to kill you, bitch," he shouted, lurching toward her.

"Hey! Get in!" a woman called from a silver sedan a few feet away. She leaned across her front seat to push the passenger car door open for Giana.

Giana didn't hesitate. She threw herself into the bucket

seat and slammed the door closed. As she searched desperately for the lock button on the unfamiliar car, she ordered, "Drive!"

The woman hit the gas, lurching them both against the seat backs. Giana twisted to look through the back window and saw Tom staggering to his car. He would be after them in a few seconds. A warning tone resounded inside the car, making her jump. Completely stressed, Giana struggled to process what threatened her now.

"Buckle your seatbelt," the woman ordered. "I'll head to the police station, but it's about ten minutes away. He'll catch us before then."

"Can I use your phone? I'll call 911." Giana struggled to secure the seatbelt as she continued to watch for Tom.

"I don't have one."

"He smashed mine. Head for the military base. It's closer. Crap! I see the front of his car." Giana struggled to hold it together.

"Give me directions," the driver demanded.

"Turn right at the next stop sign. It's about two miles down this road. Thank you for stopping."

"That wasn't going to end well."

"Yeah. You're the lady from my apartment building."

"I didn't think you'd ever seen me," the woman said, glancing sideways at Giana. "I saw those muscular guys moving you out. Military, huh?"

"My boyfriend's team. I'm Giana, by the way."

"Brooklyn. He's gaining on us."

Giana turned back. She could see Tom's face through his windshield now. Rage contorted his expression. Shaking, she drew upon all her training for emergencies to hold herself together and think proactively.

"Start honking your horn. The more attention on us, the better," Giana told Brooklyn.

"I try to avoid people noticing me, if at all possible," Brooklyn said.

Giana could hear a quiver in her rescuer's voice for the first time. She guessed immediately Brooklyn had a reason for being a ghost. "I'm sorry for getting you involved in this. Unfortunately, we're going to have to get help to survive this jerk. People may call the police to help us if they figure out we're not joyriding."

Brooklyn swallowed hard and nodded. She smashed her hand down on the steering wheel, blaring the strident horn.

Giana could see heads turning in the other cars. The woman in the car next to her glanced over. Giana held up nine fingers and then one twice over and over, hoping the woman would call for them. The older woman slowed and turned into a parking lot. Giana suspected she wouldn't help.

Another car pulled up beside them. They were a couple of teenage boys. They looked disappointed that the women weren't street racers. Giana rolled down the window and yelled for him to call 911. The passenger lifted his phone and tapped the screen.

Tom was relentless. He stayed dangerously close on their tail as he alternated between waving them over and attempting to push them off the road. Brooklyn's white-knuckled hands gripped the steering wheel as Giana braced herself on the dash.

"I'm so sorry, Brooklyn," Giana told her. "The base is a minute ahead of us. Be ready to turn right at the entrance. Stop at the gate and roll down your window. Here it is. Turn!"

"It says authorized personnel only!"

"We'll be authorized as soon as I talk to them."

Brooklyn skidded to a stop. The guards met her abrupt arrival with immediate suspicion and force. When Tom raced in behind them, they surrounded the cars with their weapons drawn. The original two must have sounded an alarm because two heavily armed men appeared in full body armor.

"Call Koa Lokela. Jerico Adams's Special Forces team. Then 911. This guy's threatening us," Giana said through her window, holding her hands up where the men could see them.

"She's delusional. That's my girlfriend. I found out that she'd been cheating. I need to talk to her alone," Tom yelled, getting out of the driver's seat of his car to stomp toward Brooklyn's.

"Stop right there, sir. Get back in your car while we figure out what's going on," a guard directed.

"I'll just grab her and go." Tom took a step forward, and the guards quickly took him down to the ground. As they were handcuffing the struggling jerk, Koa and his team arrived at a full running pace. They stopped at the sight of the last guard aiming at the women's car.

"Giana has clearance to be on base. She's mine," Koa told the last guard, who focused on the two women.

"ID?" the guard requested, not taking his eyes off Brooklyn and Giana.

Immediately, Koa showed him his. "Where's yours, Giana?"

"In my phone case. He smashed it in the apartment parking lot," she told him. All Giana wanted to do was get close to him, but couldn't until Koa defused the situation for her.

"I'll come to you in a minute, Flame. You're safe now. We're not going to let anything happen to you," Koa told her before focusing on the guard. "Can I get her out of the car, away from her attacker yet?"

"Go ahead. Your story jives with hers. I don't know this other woman. Will you vouch for her?" the guard asked.

Koa looked at Giana.

"She's a good person, Koa. She put herself at risk to save me," Giana assured him.

"I'll vouch for her," Caden interrupted. "Go get Giana, Koa." He held out his ID for the guard.

Koa immediately sped around the car. Giana opened the door and fell out into his arms. She wrapped her entire body around him, eliminating any space. Koa turned her away from the scene as Tom bellowed threats. The guards strong-armed him into the back of a military police car. The slam of the door abruptly muted his words.

"You okay, little girl?"

Relief flooded through her at the feel of his steady heartbeat against her. "Koa! I don't know what he planned to do to me. Tom appeared out of nowhere."

"Did he hurt you?" Koa's hands roamed over her back, checking for injuries. "Let me see the front of you, Giana." He peeled her off and stood her in front of him.

Zale appeared at her side as Koa checked to make sure she was okay. "Did he hurt you, Giana?"

"I'm okay, Zale," she rushed to assure him, standing patiently as Koa made sure. "He twisted my wrist, trying to pull me to his car, but that's all. I'm fine."

Zale immediately held out his hand for hers. He examined her arm quickly, asking a couple of questions and making her move it. "Just a strain. I'll grab an elastic bandage from the first-aid kit."

"I recognize that guy. He's the jerk from the fire station, right?" Koa asked.

"It's Tom Stevens. He worked at the fire station with me. He was there on the day you visited. I reassigned him to station four."

Flashing lights caught Giana's attention. The city police pulled into the entrance and met with the guards. They quickly walked over to Brooklyn's car as Zale reappeared at her side to wrap the supportive material around her hand.

"What's Caden doing?" she asked Koa.

"It appears he's protecting Brooklyn," Koa suggested.

Surprised, Giana asked, "Do they know each other?" How weird would that be if he'd met the reclusive woman?

"I don't think so," Zale answered. "Daddies sometimes go into overdrive when they see someone who needs support. Brooklyn must have given off that vibe to Caden."

Caden stood silently next to the young woman who'd saved her. She was glad Brooklyn had someone in her corner.

When Brooklyn turned and waved a hand at Giana, Koa told her, "You're next to be interviewed."

He was right. Turns out the police had received numerous calls from drivers on the road, reporting a car chase. When Giana identified herself as a fire captain who supervised the man locked in the military police cruiser, the officer quickly called for a supervisor. Giana had worked with that superior officer.

It took a while for them to gather all the necessary information and transfer Tom into a squad car. Giana could see his flapping mouth still shouting back at her as they drove away. What had she done to create this much anger?

"Are you okay, Giana?" Koa asked, hugging her to his side.

"He hates me so much. I don't have a clue why? I think that's the scariest part," she told him.

"I'm sorry, Flame. This shouldn't have happened. Don't you have a psychological screening along with physical qualifications?" Koa asked.

"We do. He passed with flying colors. I check everyone who works at my station." Giana shook herself and stepped back into fire captain mode. "I'll have to call my supervisor. He's not going to believe this."

"He wasn't in a blue car, Flame."

"I noticed that too. I think he had a tracker on my truck."

"The team will take care of that," Koa assured her. "Are you okay to go back to work?"

"I'll have to be. Thank you for being here."

"Do you need me to come with you?" he asked.

"No. This is my job. I need to stand on my own feet. It will be a long time before I get back home."

"Call me and I'll come pick you up," Koa suggested.

"I'd like that. Could you all pick up my truck from the apartment complex? I don't ever want to go there again," she admitted, shaking her head.

"Of course. Keys?"

Giana reached into her pocket, but the wrap on her hand stopped her. "Can you get it?" she asked, offering him her hip.

"My pleasure, Flame." His fingers brushed over her thigh and the side of her freshly shaved mound. Her mind instantly focused on the feelings he started inside her with the brief touch.

He gave her a wink as he pulled the key free of her jeans.

"You did that on purpose," she accused.

"Guilty as charged. Just something more appealing to focus on, little girl," he said quietly to her.

"I need to say something to Brooklyn. I think she's leaving."

Giana walked around the car and wrapped her arms around Brooklyn. "Thank you," she breathed in the other woman's ear. "I owe you one."

Stepping back, she asked Koa, "Could you find a piece of paper for me to write my phone number down on?" He nodded and ran to the guard station.

"Brooklyn, I want you to call me if you need anything." Giana held her gaze until the quiet woman nodded.

"Here, Giana. I added your contact information and mine as well, in case it takes a while for you to get a new phone," Koa told her.

"Good idea," Giana said.

Caden snagged the paper and pen before Giana could hand it over. He jotted his phone number down as well. "Call me first," he ordered. A moment later, he stepped in front of Brooklyn and shielded her from the reporters who had arrived. His muscular form protected Brooklyn from their videos and photographs.

"Let's get you out of here." Caden pulled off his sunglasses and perched them on Brooklyn's face. "Zale? Got a mask?"

"On it," Zale answered. He was back in a minute with a white mask.

Caden helped Brooklyn further disguise herself. "You're as safe as possible. Take the long way home and make sure no one is following you."

"Thank you, Caden. Could I ask you to drive my car out of here? I think they'll swarm the car," Brooklyn asked in a trembling voice.

"I'm so sorry you were dragged into this," Giana told her. She didn't know what the woman's story was, but it was something serious.

"Let's go. Get in the passenger seat and keep your head down," Caden recommended. He moved with Brooklyn to the driver's door, and she crawled over the console to huddle on the floor.

Caden leaned in to listen to something the mysterious young woman said and nodded. He glanced up at Giana and Koa. "Brooklyn wants you to be happy." His tone echoed with sadness. Usually stoic and focused, Caden's face softened for a split second. He slid into the driver's seat and navigated out of the crowd.

Giana met Koa's gaze. He didn't need to say anything. He'd seen his senior teammate's expression as well.

"Your car is here to take you to the station," Koa said, pointing to a fire department vehicle on the far side of the assembled crowd. He turned to his team. "Protection detail?"

The men formed a wall around her. Giana stayed in the middle and remained silent as they escorted her to the waiting car. The reporters pelted her with questions, trying to figure out who she was. As Giana expected, they followed her.

Giana spent hours coordinating with her supervisors before finally making a statement to the media. Of course, she got to add to her microphone collection. Surely by now, the news station charged the super pushy reporter for each one she lost.

As the day progressed, she reminded herself frequently that Koa would come get her soon and help her escape from this shit show. Thank goodness she had Koa. Thank goodness she had her daddy.

CHAPTER 18

Koa brought his stressed-out little girl directly to her nursery after ushering her inside. She loved to play in the fully outfitted and decorated room. It was her solace and recovery spot when life got crazy.

He rocked Giana on his lap. She held Tiger and Jellybean tight to her chest with her head resting on his shoulder. The stuffies seemed to reassure her she was safe. After several long quiet moments, he finally felt the tension ease from her muscles. "Good girl. Just relax."

"This was a horrible day."

"It was," he commiserated with her. Koa had stewed for the rest of the day, plotting Tom's demise in a number of gruesome ways. Thank goodness for his team's efforts to burn off his anger and frustration. Jerico had stepped up to take on the training lead position since Caden hadn't returned to work out with them. He'd chosen to shield Brooklyn from the media storm.

"I was so scared, but I didn't let Tom know that. I don't know how he hid all that anger inside for so long," she worried.

"He obviously has problems. I doubt you were the first person he's targeted. But now, he's shown his true self. He can't hide anymore."

"The fire department suspended him immediately. Human resources folks will work with the lawyers to protect the department. The firefighters are pissed. A few admitted that he'd said some weird things about me over the last few months. They felt guilty for not warning me, but had chalked it up to awkward guy ramblings."

"Do you think they'll come to you if something seems weird in the future?" Koa asked, trying to squash the flash of anger that speared him at the thought that others had not spoken up.

"I think so. I have a meeting with the shift leaders tomorrow to create a plan to help everyone recover after this. Tom's anger was targeted at me, but shared risk and experiences bond together firefighters. We'll work on creating more open lines of communication and rebuilding trust."

"Will it help you?"

"It will." Giana was quiet for a moment before adding, "What helped me the most was having you in my life. I knew you would support me through this. I've hesitated to tell you this because I wanted to be sure."

Koa swallowed hard. He hoped he knew what she would say.

"I love you, Daddy."

"Say that again, little girl," he demanded, feeling moisture fill his eyes.

"I love you, Daddy. I'm sorry I didn't say it…"

Interrupting her, Koa lifted her torso up to press against his as he kissed her with every ounce of passion in his heart. They were both breathing heavily when he lifted his lips from hers.

"I love you so much, Giana. You're the little girl I always dreamed of finding and the woman who completes my life."

She lifted her mouth to his. Koa let her lead the kiss until the heat threatened to become too much. He still needed to take care of something.

He forced himself to lean away from her slightly. "Before I fuck every last worry out of your mind, I think you need something else."

"What do I need?" Giana asked, rubbing her breasts on his chest.

"A reminder to follow directions. If you'd simply jumped in your truck when you finished the paperwork, Tom would not have had the opportunity to approach you."

"Coulda, shoulda, woulda. I couldn't have anticipated this happening, Daddy."

"But you could have avoided it."

Giana opened her mouth to argue and hesitated. She sighed deeply and nodded. "You're right. Are you going to spank me?" she asked, giving him sad puppy eyes and a pouting lower lip.

Koa kept himself from grinning at his cute little girl. She was adorable. "Ten minutes in the corner."

"Oh. That doesn't sound too bad." She leaned forward and kissed his cheek.

"Wearing a naughty girl plug in your bottom," he added and watched her eagerness deflate.

"That's mean, Daddy."

"Punishment is supposed to help you remember to make better choices. Go get the black case on the shelf."

"Couldn't you just give me a stern talking-to? You could yell at me like a recruit. I bet that would stick with me."

"I'm never going to yell at you. The black case, little girl. You can leave Tiger and Jellybean with me. I'll stuffie sit."

Moving as slowly as a sloth, Giana slid from his lap and

surrendered her stuffies. After crossing the room, she lifted a hand to touch the case and turned to meet his gaze as if she hoped he'd change his mind. He treasured every part of her, but her resistance followed by her submission got him. She chose every time to be his little girl.

"Bring it to me, Flame."

She dropped her gaze from his and dragged the case off the shelf. Returning at a snail's pace, she held the case away from her body. "Here, Daddy. Since I've never had corner time, maybe I should ease into it. You know, no plug the first time."

"Who's in charge, little girl?"

Seconds passed as she scuffed her bare toes into the thick carpet. "Daddy," she whispered.

"Good girl. I'm very proud of you for accepting your punishment. You're going to feel better soon."

"Promise?"

"I promise." Koa set the case on his lap and considered the plugs. He ran his finger down the largest and heard her gasp. Keeping his expression serious, he said, "This isn't usually for a punishment. I'll use it to prepare you to take Daddy in your bottom. My little girl needs a reminder to follow directions."

He ran his fingers down the row of plugs, considering each one. Her gaze felt almost physical on his hand. Koa stopped at the second smallest plug and pulled it out of the case. Her shoulders sagged in relief. He plucked the tube of lubricant from the case as well and shut it with a snap.

Setting it beside the rocker, Koa stood the items in his hands on the small table nearby. He drew her between his thighs and asked, "What is Daddy punishing you for, little girl?"

"I put myself in danger because I let curiosity overwhelm my need to be safe."

"I like how you said that, Flame. Curiosity is a good thing. It helps us learn. But be curious in a safe situation."

"Yes, Daddy. Can you punish me now, Daddy?"

"Let's get your clothes off. Little girls stand in the corner nude."

She nodded as if she accepted that. He quickly tugged off the big T-shirt he'd changed her into when he'd gotten her home. Her smiling cloud panties landed on top of the discarded garment quickly.

"Let me help you, little girl," he whispered in her ear.

Giana nodded and hugged him impetuously. He kissed her forehead before lifting her over his knees. Koa stifled a groan as her full hips brushed across his rigidly stiff cock. As soon as she was in the corner, he'd unzip his pants. For now, he balanced her across his knees and rubbed her adorable bottom.

"Relax, little girl. Lubricant first," he reminded her. Koa loved the single-use, small tubes of lubricant with the applicator tip. Snapping off the top with an audible click, Koa watched her jump at the sound. He spread her buttocks and paused for a moment to admire her alluring body.

"Daddy," she whimpered and hid her face against his thigh.

"Little girls don't rush their daddies," he reminded her, tapping the center of her tightly clenched opening. "Relax your muscles, Flame. I don't want to hurt you."

Koa waited patiently. Finally, the tension eased from her cute bottom. Koa squeezed the tube to apply some of the mixture to her opening before pressing the applicator tip into her bottom and squeezing it fully. His little girl squirmed at the feel of the mixture gushing into her tight channel.

Setting the tube aside, he smoothed the thick mixture

into place. Her bottom was very sensitive and always responded to his touch. He pressed his finger deep into her slowly, letting her feel every millimeter of the digit.

Koa held his finger implanted in her without moving it as her breath quickened. Her upper thighs glistened with arousal. He could help her climax in a moment.

"Move, Daddy!" she pleaded.

"This is punishment, little girl. Not pleasure."

"I don't get to come?" she wailed.

"At the end of your punishment, if you've been a good girl, Daddy will reward you." Koa assured her.

She nodded and drooped over his lap, submitting completely to his authority. "I'll be good."

Koa turned his inserted finger left and right, spreading the mixture. When he was satisfied that he'd prepared her, he removed his finger and pressed the tip of the plug to her opening. The cold metal glided on a sea of lubricant as he pressed it inside slowly. Koa stopped when it reached the fullest part and allowed it to glide back out. He teased her three more times, making sure her attention focused completely on his efforts.

The fifth time he stopped at the widest part, Koa said, "Ask me to fill your bottom with the plug, little girl."

She looked over her shoulder to make sure she'd heard him correctly. Koa nodded his head. "Go ahead, Giana. Ask Daddy to put the plug in your bottom."

Giana swallowed hard and whispered, "Do I have to?"

"Saying it aloud will help teach you the lesson that I'd like you to learn."

He wouldn't allow her to hide from anything. She blinked her eyes closed before saying, "Daddy, I'm sorry I messed up. Please put the plug in my bottom."

"Good girl." Koa pressed the plug into place and rubbed

her bottom as she wiggled, adjusting to the feel of the thick device filling her. When she'd stilled, he instructed, "Go stand in the corner, little girl. I'll let you know when it's time to come back to Daddy."

Relying on his support to stand, Giana weaved unsteadily on her feet as each movement affected her. When she could, Giana took baby steps to the corner. She braced her forearms on the wall in front of her and rested her head on them in relief that she'd made it.

Seconds ticked by, feeling like hours. How long would he make her stand there?

Giana heard the sound of his zipper releasing. She lifted her forehead and turned to see what he was doing.

"Uh, uh, little girl. Face the wall," he corrected her before she could swivel her head even a few inches.

A groan and a whisper of movement followed his statement. Her imagination went wild. Was he stroking himself?

She could picture it in her head. His hand pulling roughly on his thick cock. A few droplets of his cum would gather on the broad tip. Giana licked her lips, wishing she could taste him. The arousal brewing inside her combusted as she squeezed her inner thighs together.

Standing in this corner was torture. She'd take a spanking anytime over this. The plug in her bottom kept her desire at a level she couldn't distract herself from. Trapped in an endless loop of desire, forcing her to shift and the plug moving inside, pushing her passion higher, Giana could feel her juices coating her pussy and inner thighs. Was it possible for her to combust?

A squeak came from the chair behind her. Giana stiffened her spine, guarding herself from turning around. She heard the whisper of footsteps on the carpet. *He's coming here!*

Warm hands wrapped around her waist, tugging her back to him. His hard cock settled along the cleft of her bottom. A hand pressed between her shoulders to pin her in place against the wall. Her arms slid down to stabilize her body now bent over at almost a ninety-degree angle.

Koa drew his fingers down her spine to her waist before trailing around to her abdomen and lower. When they reached her mound, his desire-roughened voice asked, "Little girl, have you learned your lesson?"

"Yes, Daddy! Please, touch me," she begged.

He slid his fingers into her juices and caressed her. Giana lifted her bottom offering herself to him.

"My little girl is needy. Should I reward you for taking your punishment so well?"

"Daddy, please. I need you."

Koa fit his cock to her pussy and pushed. Giana gasped as he entered. The plug filled her bottom as he thrust into her. His movement nudged the device inside her through the thin wall separating her entrances. When she thought she couldn't handle any more, his pelvis brushed her bottom.

His fingers brushed over her clit. "Can you come for me, little girl?" His hips pulsed forward slowly, rocking her against the wall as he caressed her.

The whirl of sensations inside and around her overwhelmed her. With a cry, Giana exploded. The hard climax rocked her. Her knees trembled as she struggled to stand through the pleasure. Koa's powerful arm wrapped under her stomach, holding her tight.

As soon as she caught her breath, he withdrew and thrust forward. The sinuous feel of his powerful frame wrapped around her as he filled her captivated Giana. Focusing only on the pleasure he rebuilt inside her, she abandoned all thoughts. Koa forced her to feel—to live for this moment only.

When he finally allowed himself to come, Giana felt

completely boneless. Somehow, she found herself back on his lap as he rocked her to sleep.

"Empty," she whispered.

"Daddy will fill you again, Flame."

She nodded and rested her cheek on his hard chest. Her daddy always kept his word.

EPILOGUE

*A*s they walked back into the house after a thrilling excursion, Giana said, "I had a fun day at the zoo, Daddy. Thank you for taking me and Tiger to see his cousins. Those giraffes are so tall. Do you think Tiger will grow anymore?"

"I think Tiger is happy being stuffie-sized. He couldn't fit in our bed if he was zoo-animal sized."

"Good point. That wouldn't work at all. Do you think the birds ate all the giraffe cookies we rescued from that box?" She and Koa had searched carefully through the assortment of animal crackers. When she'd lined them up next to the fence at the safari section of the zoo, a ton of birds had swooped in to munch on them. Koa had pulled her away when she'd tried to rescue them. "That was an incredibly mean crow."

"He had no manners at all. The birds did show us that it was okay to eat the giraffes," Koa pointed out.

"Tiger didn't care at all that they gobbled them up. He told me I was silly to worry about crackers. I guess it's okay for me to eat them from now on."

"That's a very scientific conclusion, little girl. That will also keep us from being thrown out of the zoo for feeding the animals."

"So many birds swooped in! I've never seen a swarm like that," Giana admitted, and a giggle escaped from her mouth. "You yanked me away from the one that tried to peck me so fast!"

"I'll always protect you, Flame. Even from yourself," Koa told her with a loving smile.

"Thanks, Daddy."

"Come here, you. I need a cuddle to help my heart recover from the scare of that menacing crow and all his buddies." Koa picked up Giana and sat down on the couch, holding her close. She laid her head on his shoulder and relaxed, getting lost in her own thoughts.

Thank goodness everything had settled down now that Tom was in jail. Giana kept thinking about the woman who'd saved her. During the investigation, they'd discovered Tom hadn't trashed her apartment. He had an air-tight alibi. He'd actually been at the firehouse according to the schedule and numerous witnesses.

The police had spotted the blue sedan on the video footage of the parking lot. That rude man had entered behind a resident that evening. Only one person in the building had recognized him. Brooklyn. She'd admitted to being on the run from her stepfather after her mother's death. This revelation led the authorities to suggest the man had busted into the wrong apartment.

"I'm worried about Brooklyn. No one should have to live like that."

"Caden texted a few minutes ago that she was staying in his guest room for a while," Koa shared.

Giana pushed away from his chest to meet his gaze.

"Really? He invited someone he didn't know to sleep at his house?"

"I think Caden knows everything he needs to know about Brooklyn."

"He thinks she is his Little, doesn't he?"

"You're getting a few steps ahead of everyone, Giana. Caden knows she needs help. He's interested in helping. Perhaps having him standing behind her will convince the stepfather to change his intentions. Would you mess with Caden?"

"No way. I mean, of all the guys, Max is bigger, but Caden's the toughest," Giana said.

"And I'm chopped liver?" Koa asked, pretending to be offended.

"You're the Daddiest?"

"That will get you back on my good girl list," Koa said with a wink.

"Perfect. Can we invite her over here or go see her soon?" Giana asked.

"I think we'll see a lot of Brooklyn in the future. Give her a bit of time to settle in with Caden."

"Yes, Daddy."

Koa kissed her on the forehead and stood to walk into the kitchen. He pulled steaks out of the refrigerator to season them. "How do you like your steak cooked? Medium? I like mine medium rare."

"You're going to grill, Daddy?" she asked hesitantly.

"I won't burn them," he said, scowling at her as he washed his hands.

"Medium rare is fine, Daddy," she assured him before asking, "Where did you put that fire extinguisher I ordered?"

He rolled his eyes and dragged the shiny new canister from under the sink. "Come on, my little fire captain. You can sit by the grill."

She popped up from the couch and set Jelly and Tiger safely on the cushions. They'd be safe inside. She skipped to her daddy and took the extinguisher from him. Better safe than sorry.

"Ouch!" she yelped when his hand smacked her bottom on the way to the door. His deep laughter rolled over her, inspiring her to giggle as well. Teasing Daddy came with consequences.

The End

AFTERWORD

Stormy Night Publications would like to thank you for your interest in our books.

If you liked this book (or even if you didn't), we would really appreciate you leaving a review on the site where you purchased it. Reviews provide useful feedback for us and our authors, and this feedback (both positive comments and constructive criticism) allows us to work even harder to make sure we provide the content our customers want to read.

If you would like to check out more books from Stormy Night Publications, if you want to learn more about our company, or if you would like to join our mailing list, please visit our website at:

http://www.stormynightpublications.com

BOOKS OF THE SOLDIER DADDIES SERIES

The Medic's Little Girl

When stern, handsome army medic Doniphan Williams asks her out, it isn't long before twenty-three-year-old waitress River Reynolds blushingly admits her need for a firm-handed daddy. But daddies expect to be obeyed, and when River doesn't keep in touch as instructed while Doniphan is away on a mission she quickly ends up over his knee for a sound spanking on her bare bottom.

As she is held in Doniphan's arms after her punishment, River feels more safe and loved than she ever has before, and when he claims her properly it is more pleasurable than she could have ever imagined. Soon she is quivering with need as he takes her temperature and gives her a thorough, intimate examination, but will she be a good girl for daddy even when he puts her in diapers?

Tex's Little Girl

When a big, strong, handsome soldier tells off a customer who was treating her poorly, pastry chef Rosie Perez soon finds herself baking cookies for her rescuer… and calling him daddy.

Tex is the kind of daddy who will cuddle her when she's upset. He's also the kind who will take his little girl over his knee and spank her bare bottom very soundly when she's been naughty, then bathe her and put her to bed in her nursery to remind her that she's not a big girl anymore.

Though Rosie blushes crimson as Tex diapers her for the first time, when he takes her in his arms and claims her properly it is the most pleasure she has ever experienced. But when she has to visit the doctor will she be a good girl for daddy or will her bottom be bright red for her exam?

Jax's Little Girl

Jax Wescott isn't the kind of man who ignores a woman in need of assistance, and when he witnesses Ember Stevens having a panic attack in a park he gently helps her through it. But it quickly becomes clear that Ember is in need of quite a bit more than just a hug and a pep talk.

She needs a daddy. A daddy who will not just take care of her, but take charge of her as well.

A daddy like Jax.

Though she sobs as she is spanked very soundly on her bare bottom for being reckless with her safety and blushes crimson when she is put to bed in a nursery, being held in Jax's arms and claimed properly is better than she could have ever dreamed. But will she behave herself when the time comes for daddy to take her to the doctor for a very thorough, embarrassing exam?

Sam's Little Girl

As she enjoys her cotton candy at the state fair the last thing twenty-two-year-old Hope Anderson expects is to end up riding the Ferris wheel with a handsome special ops soldier who calls her little girl, but Sam Memphis knows a woman in need of a daddy when he sees one.

Hope soon learns the hard way that Sam meant what he said about naughty girls getting a sound spanking, and it isn't long before she's being put in a diaper with her bottom still bright red. She delights in every moment of her daddy's intimate attention even when it leaves her blushing, but will a visit to the doctor for a very thorough exam prove more embarrassing than she can bear?

The Captain's Little Girl

Though Captain Mark Cunningham has wanted beautiful waitress Cricket Wilson to be his little girl for years, he's old enough to be her father and he's always told himself he isn't right for her. But when the battle-hardened special forces officer barely makes it home alive from a dangerous assignment, he decides it is time to do what he should have done ages ago and claim her as his.

Cricket is delighted when the handsome soldier she's dreamed about for so long finally takes her in his arms, and no matter how bright red she blushes she has never felt safer and more loved than when he bathes her, puts her in diapers, and even brings her to the medic for a very intimate exam. But when a mission puts her new daddy behind enemy lines will she lose him forever?

Jerico's Little Girl

Twenty-five-year-old Aspen Randolph has always dreamed of a big, strong daddy who would take her in hand and make sure she feels safe and loved, and when special forces officer Jerico Adams steps in to rescue her from a threatening situation her dream suddenly becomes reality.

But Jerico doesn't just plan to make Aspen's troubles his business. He plans to make her his.

Sometimes that will mean spanking her when she's naughty, then bathing her and putting her down for a nap with her bottom still stinging. Other times it will mean bringing her to the doctor for a thorough examination, or even putting her in diapers despite how bright red she blushes.

Most of all, though, it means she can trust daddy to take care of her no matter what.

Zale's Little Girl

After gorgeous army medic Zale Reynolds saves Pippa Twinner from a kidnapper, he doesn't just bring her home with him and make it his business to take care of her. He makes her call him daddy too.

Though she blushes crimson as her ruggedly handsome rescuer bathes her, puts her to bed, and takes her temperature the old-fashioned way, Pippa cherishes his loving attention, and when he takes her over his knee and spanks her bare bottom, she doesn't just promise to be a very good girl for her new daddy.

She comes really hard for him too.

MORE STORMY NIGHT BOOKS BY PEPPER NORTH

A Polar Hope (included in *Marked Brides: Six Alpha Shifter Romances*)

After losing her job on Earth, Marisol signs up for a cultural exchange program with Terra Arcus, but upon her arrival she is stripped and put up for auction. When the northern clan chief recognizes her as his own, he claims her and escorts her back to his lands. While their future children are the hope for the clan's survival, she captures her stern mate's heart as well. He will ease her adaptation to her new life with a firm hand and a loving embrace.

A Polar Second Chance (included in *Claimed Brides: Seven Alpha Shifter Romances*)

Ruth would have never expected to experience a connection with the seer of Clan Thorben, but merely touching the handsome polar bear shifter's hand leaves her feeling warm in a way she never has before. But he doesn't plan for her to be just his mate. She will be his little girl also, to be loved, cherished, and spanked very soundly on her bare bottom when she's been naughty.

PEPPER NORTH LINKS

You can keep up with Pepper North via her website, her Twitter account, her Facebook page, her Amazon page, and her Goodreads profile, using the following links:

https://4peppernorth.club/
https://twitter.com/4peppernorth
https://www.facebook.com/PepperNorthauthor
https://www.amazon.com/stores/Pepper-North/author/B072MWDRD4
https://www.goodreads.com/author/show/16941120.Pepper_North

Printed in Dunstable, United Kingdom